Peter Wrigley, alias 'Worm', is small, nervous and unpopular—a perfect target for bullies. His life at home and at school is pretty miserable and he dreams of doing something important that will prove he's not really a wimp. Unfortunately his attempt to save the school is a complete farce and only makes things worse.

Then a walking holiday in the Lake District changes everything. Although spoiled and bossy 'Pig' Baxter joins the trip, he's determined to have a good time. And when Pig does something really stupid, Worm finds himself facing the greatest challenge of his life—an adventure which will really show what he's made of!

ANN PILLING has published several adult fiction titles and more than a dozen children's novels, including *Henry's Leg*, which won the Guardian Award for Children's Fiction. She lives in Oxford with her husband.

DAVID PITHER?

The Year of the Worm

For Dorothy Edwards,
in affectionate and grateful memory

ANN PILLING

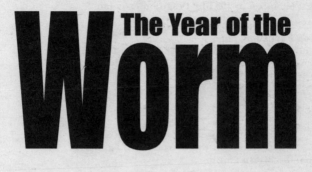

The Year of the
Worm

LION
Children's Books

First published in 1984 by Penguin Books Ltd

This edition published by
Lion Publishing plc
Sandy Lane West, Oxford, England
www.lion-publishing.co.uk
ISBN 0 7459 4294 6

This edition 2000
10 9 8 7 6 5 4 3 2 1 0

A catalogue record for this book is available
from the British Library

Typeset in 10.25/12 Baskerville BT
Printed and bound in Great Britain
by Omnia Books Ltd

It may be doubted whether there are many other animals which have played so important a part in the history of the world as have these lowly organized creatures.

Charles Darwin, writing about worms in
The Formation of Vegetable Mould, 1881

1

When the postman knocked on the door, Patsy got there first and opened it. But Worm was behind her, still in his vest and underpants. He grabbed the parcel and rushed upstairs, throwing it on the bed while he hunted round for a pair of scissors. Soon he had cut the string, slit through the Sellotape, and ripped off the brown paper. Then, from the flat box inside, he pulled out the glittering apparatus.

As he gripped the handles a piece of paper fluttered to the floor. Worm sat down on his bed and looked at it. The man on the leaflet looked like Tarzan. He had gigantic muscles, a chest like a hairy doormat, and a toothpaste smile. The balloon coming from his mouth said: 'Within *one week* you will *feel* and *look* inches taller. With very little effort *you too* can have a *body like mine*. Be the envy of your friends. Just follow these simple exercises, and *do as I do*.'

The simple exercises were printed in very small letters. Worm stood up, took a deep breath, and pulled. Nothing happened. He clenched his teeth, stood on his toes and tried again. This time his hands moved apart about a quarter of an inch. But it was hard work. His arms felt as if someone was pulling them out of their sockets, his head swam horribly, and he felt faint.

He was just *not fit*. He sat down on the bed again and decided to read the instructions more carefully.

It was Monday morning. At twenty past eight his mother shouted up the stairs, 'Peter! If you're not down here in two minutes this breakfast's going in the bin!' But Worm was still in his underwear, and when his sister came up to fetch him for school he was standing red-faced in front of the mirror, trying to do Exercise One with his new chest-expanders.

'Don't know how you can read that, Peter, not when you're so late,' his mother called through from the back kitchen, where she was sorting out washing.

Worm stared at the photograph on the front page of the *Darnley Examiner*. TWO BRAVE CHILDREN ran the headline and it said underneath: 'The Mayor of Darnley, Councillor William Hobbs, welcomed two brave children to the Town Hall on Saturday and presented each of them with a certificate and a special bravery medal.'

Still reading, Worm pulled on his kagoule and picked up his school bag. The girl had jumped into a canal and saved a toddler from drowning; the boy had leapt from a third-floor window with his baby sister when their flat caught fire. He was only eleven.

Worm thought about them as he walked to school with Patsy. *He* wanted to do something brave. He'd been planning it for a long time now. The idea had taken root three years ago, the day his mother had said to him, 'You're the man of the house now, Peter.' It was after Dad died.

He was a lorry driver for Baxter's Spring Works and he'd been killed in a very bad accident on the M6 motorway. Baxter's sent Mum money every month, but it wasn't much. So she'd gone back to what she was doing before she married Dad, running a fish and chip shop.

They were good, Wrigley's chips, everyone said so, but she had to work hard, and there wasn't much money left over when all the bills were paid. Worm had saved up for months to buy those chest-expanders.

Now they'd arrived he was going to get really fit. In the two weeks left before the Easter holidays he planned to get up early each morning to do his exercises. Then he was going youth-hostelling in the Lake District. All that mountain walking would be bound to strengthen his leg muscles. When they got back he might go in for the qualifying heats of the Great Moorland Race, a charity-run for school children. The Darnley Harriers were planning it for July. If an eight-mile slog across the moors didn't get him fit, then nothing would.

• THE MOST COURAGEOUS YOUNGSTER IN DARNLEY. He could already see the huge newspaper headline floating in front of him, and there he was, in the photograph, going up to receive his medal. Nobody would say he smelt of fish and chips then, nobody would laugh at his clothes. And it wouldn't be the Mayor of Darnley waiting on the Town Hall steps. It would be the Queen.

'T'ra Peter,' Patsy said, turning into the gates of her Junior School. Darnley Comprehensive was at the end of the same road, and the clock was striking. 'T'ra,' Peter said, and started to run.

Patsy was the only person who didn't call him Worm, apart from his mother. He hated it, but he was lumbered with it now. He'd had it for too long. Mum was always telling him that only popular people got nicknames, but Worm wasn't popular. He was small, pale, and nervous. He never walked down the middle of a corridor but crept along the side, waiting for kicks.

He'd liked it in the Junior School but at the Comprehensive work was much harder and he was near the bottom of the class. Nobody bothered about that if you were good at a sport, but Worm wasn't, he was too thin and weedy. He didn't seem to have grown much since he was Patsy's age. She was only seven but she'd be as tall as he was soon.

'Waiting for a spurt, that's all you're doing,' Mum said reassuringly. 'You'll shoot up one of these days, just you see.' But he was still waiting.

It was in Class One Infants that he'd got the name Worm, during Music and Movement. Six years ago it was, when he was five. He could still hear Miss Dixon's high scrapy voice: 'Now, children, listen carefully, and when the music changes remember you're not *flowers* any more, you're *worms*, little wriggly *worms*. Listen for the music *and*—'

'Wriggly, wriggly *worms*!' all the children had squealed in delight. 'Wriggly! Peter Wrigley! Peter Wrigley *Worm*!' And the one shouting loudest was a boy called Frankie Hudd. He'd been in Worm's class since that very first day, and they were still together at the Comprehensive. He had a nickname too, they called him Frud. Nobody laughed at him though; he was clever.

Frud was the only real friend Worm had. He belonged to the Darnley Rambling Club with his dad and his older brother, Graham, and they were all mad about wildlife. They spent most of their spare time birdwatching up on the moors above Darnley. It was Graham who'd organized the Lake District trip.

Worm didn't really blame Frud for what he'd done in Class One Infants, when they were being worms for Miss Dixon. Things like that just happened. If he'd grown a bit more, and not been so whey-faced and skinny, the name might not have stuck. *Worm.* Hanging on the very edge of groups in case he got laughed at. *Worm.* Thin and squashy and soft in the middle. *Worm.* The boy who was bullied from his very first day, the boy who never stood up to anyone. All his clothes looked about ten sizes too big. Even his underpants had to be turned up. *Worm.* You could see how he'd got saddled with it.

Not for much longer though. As he ran into school he thought of the chest-expanders waiting on his bed. He would be up those mountains in a couple of weeks. All the poking fun would be a thing of the past soon. He'd be in training.

2

Last lesson on Mondays was English with the student. His name was Mr Ferris but he said they could call him Simon. He wore corduroy suits and shirts with jazzy stripes on, and very old sneakers. The class thought he was lazy. The lesson was supposed to be English Language but he'd re-christened it Creative Writing and spent most of the time reading up at the front while the children worked on their own.

Worm dreaded it. English was his worst subject and the things the student dreamed up for them to do were quite impossible. Last week, for example, he'd chalked up the word CHAOS on the blackboard in gigantic letters. 'Let's see what you can do with that,' he'd said. 'Write a story, or a poem. Just let your imagination *take off*!' Then he'd fished a book out of his pocket and made himself comfortable at the teacher's table.

Simon always said the same things and Frud had started to compile a teacher's phrase-book. 'Quickly and quietly' was one favourite, 'Settle down now' other. 'Let your imagination *take off*!' had just been added. When he thought of CHAOS Worm's imagination felt about as mobile as a wet lettuce.

There was always a chatty five minutes at the beginning to discuss what they were going to write. Today the student announced, 'I want you to invent a *Year*, to celebrate something you think is important. You all know the kind of thing, I'm sure. We've had the Year of the Child, and the Year of the Disabled. Well, that's all very interesting. But now it's your turn. I want something really exciting from you today. *Let yourselves go!*'

That was quite a good one for the list. Worm could see Frud quietly smiling to himself and getting the phrase-book out.

'*Right*,' the student said briskly (there went another one). 'No, no, hands *down*' (there was only one hand *up*). He walked round the classroom dishing paper out. 'You've got something to write on, now just get down to it. Be original. You might come up with something really inspiring.'

Worm stared down glumly at his piece of paper, feeling as inspired as a lead balloon. Heck, it was worse than CHAOS. The student had put his feet up on the table and had started to read. Teaching wasn't a bad life, if you got organized. The book was called *The Claws of Darkness*. On the cover was a picture of a man in a pith helmet being sucked into a swamp. He was already half-eaten by a grinning monster.

Worm stared out of the window. All round him people were scratching away with their pens. In the next desk Frud wrote rapidly. He'd already filled half a page with his small neat script. He'd be going on about birds, the Year of the Lesser Spotted M

Warbler, or something. On the other side Sonia Stevens was hard at work too. She'd be writing about the Year of the Nerds, or whichever group was at the top of the charts. All she ever thought about was pop music.

There was a lot of giggling at the back where Steve Weir sat with his gang. Worm avoided them as far as possible; that was why, after Christmas, he'd asked for a desk near the front. That lot had given him hell in his first term, poking him in the back all the time, taking single threads of his hair and pulling them, telling him he smelt of the chip shop.

He bent over his empty piece of paper and chewed his pen. In the desk behind, Terence Ackroyd was sniggering and he could hear Steve Weir issuing muffled instructions from the back row. Ackroyd shouldn't be sitting behind Worm anyway, but he'd managed to swap with a girl in row three—said he couldn't see the board or something. It was all lies.

Soon Worm knew why. He felt fingers scrabbling with his shirt and trousers, trying to make a gap, trying to expose a portion of the pale, worm-like flesh. Then, *squelch*, and he prickled with cold as he felt a big soggy lump of something slide slowly down his bare back, under his vest, something wet and dripping that sent slow trickles down into the seat of his pants.

He half stood up in his seat, got his hand round to the back, and tried to get the thing out. But whatever it was had disintegrated in transit, and Worm ended up with less than half of it. The student, vaguely aware of trouble at the back, glanced up from *The ...s of Darkness* and shifted in his chair. Worm didn't want to get told off. He sat down again abruptly. *Splat*, the wet lump had squished out between his bottom and his chair. He had squashed the mystery item flat.

Silence took over. Worm secretly inspected his fingers. Black ink all over them, and fuzzy shreds of paper tissue stuck to his nails. They'd soaked a load of paper towels in ink and made a ball of it, which had slipped down to his pants.

Mum would kill him when she found out. He'd have ink all over his trousers, and they were new. What's more they'd got to last him. His mother worried about money and she bought everything to allow room for growth. That's why he looked such a comic, with his school sweatshirt turned up at the wrists, his yawning shirt collars, and his drooping football shorts.

Now Terence Ackroyd was digging a ruler into his back. He wanted Worm to shift so that they could all see what the ink-bomb had done to his trousers. Worm wriggled and slid about in his seat, then he gave a nervous cough and looked helplessly at Frud.

Frud was already on to his second side and writing like a maniac. Worm had to cough twice before he looked up. Then their eyes met. Misery was written all over the pinched, white face and there were tears in his eyes. 'Frud,' the face was saying, '*Frud*, look what they're doing to me. *Help*.'

The back-row brigade had all leaned forward and Weir was hissing, 'Go'orn Terry, sock him one. G⊷ him out of his seat, can't you?'

Frud turned round and glared at the lot beh then he looked hard at Worm. 'For Heaven's he wanted to yell at him, 'stick up for yourself a bit. Terence Ackroyd's not all that big, what's the matter with you? Give him a thump. You'll only need to do it once and they'll leave off you in future. Don't be so *pathetic*.'

But he didn't say anything. He shoved his head down and pretended to write, but all the facts about owls had gone clean out of his head. All he could see was Worm's pleading, anguished face and the tears spilling down on to his cheeks. He felt bad, ignoring him. Worm was his friend, he'd always stuck up for Worm. But sometimes he was so feeble even Frud cringed. They were only in the first form. If Worm didn't stand up to Steve Weir's lot a bit more he'd never survive to be a second year.

Terence Ackroyd must have got bored with the ruler treatment because the poking stopped suddenly and Worm heard the ruler clatter to the floor. He relaxed slightly and began to write with a shaking hand 'The Year of the...' at the top of his piece of paper. Then the whispering started up again. Worm heard his name quite clearly, followed by a few suppressed snorts. He glanced behind him and saw a piece of paper being passed along the back row. The student looked up once again from his riveting paperback.

'Settle down now,' he said irritably (the monster had just gobbled up its third victim). 'You can't do decent work *and* chatter' (another one for Frud's list). ut the noises, much quieter, went on. Everyone was ding the paper and exploding into quiet laughter. n had a cold, tight feeling in his stomach. It was him.

He would have to make a quick getaway when the bell went. He was first in the cloakroom but (surprise, surprise) someone had pinched his kagoule. It went missing regularly, along with his football boots and half the things in his desk. After ten minutes' search he found it rolled up and stuffed into 3B's wastepaper basket. Just for once he was grateful to his mother for buying everything so big. There was room for two inside his kagoule. It came right down over his bottom and hid the ink stains.

By the time he reached the playground half the school had already gone home. He could see Patsy peering through the railings, looking for him. But he couldn't reach her. The Enemy was by the gate.

'Wait a minute, Worm!' Steve Weir called out. 'This is for you. We wrote it specially!' He was large, with a big flat face and stringy black hair like liquorice. But his voice was strangely feeble and thin. It reminded Worm of toothpaste being squeezed out of a tube.

'Leave off,' he muttered as someone stuck their foot out slyly and sent him flying.

'Come on, Worm,' Toothpaste was shouting. 'You'll enjoy this.'

He stood there miserably. The school gates were guarded by the Barrett brothers, two of Weir's cronies out of the second year, the tough guys. It was no good trying to get past them.

'I'm not listening,' he said under his breath, looking round desperately for Frud. He wouldn't b in on this. Where on earth *was* he?

'*Worms*,' Steve Weir began, climbing up on to railings so that everybody could see him pro

'Now, the question is: Do *worms* have *brains*? Most people find them repulsive, slimy slippery pink things, about as revolting as overcooked spaghetti. Worms, on the whole, are not the kind of thing you'd want to find in your bed, let alone on your plate!'

They were all laughing. The student, on his way home, climbed off his bicycle and looked up at Steve with a gratified smile. 'Go on, Weir,' he said. 'This sounds quite promising.'

Toothpaste went a bit pink. Worm was standing right next to the student, staring down scarlet-faced at the litter in the playground. Patsy was still by the railings. Suddenly, it didn't seem so funny any more.

Then an older boy called Pig Baxter shouted up from the back, 'Go on, Steve, let's hear the rest of it.'

'*Well*, I feel it's time we all took a fresh look at *worms*. After all, they may not be as weak and spineless as some people think. It's a pity the very *look* of a worm gives most people the creeps. But I suggest that Our Friend Worm is given a fair trial from now on and that this year should be called the *Year of the Worm*.'

'I like it,' the student said, getting back on his bike. 'Our Friend Worm. That's good. Write a bit more, Weir, and we'll hear it next Monday. Bye for now.' And he pedalled off through the gates.

'T'ra sir,' they all shouted. What a laugh.

But the crowd broke up in no time when the headmaster, Mr Fothergill, came out into the playground and got into his car. Worm slipped out and found Patsy. He took her hand and started to firmly down the road.

hat are you going to do, Peter, about those boys?'

'Nothing. I'm not bothered.'

'Why didn't that man tell them off?'

'*Him?*' Worm said scornfully. 'Oh, he didn't get it. He doesn't know anyone's nickname. He's on another planet, he is.' Too busy reading *The Claws of Darkness* he thought to himself as they crossed the main road.

'Don't worry, Peter,' Patsy said.

'I'm *not. And don't tell me mam.*'

3

They let themselves into the shop and went through to the sitting-room at the back. Mum was out at Auntie Glad's, two streets away. Patsy didn't like being on her own after school.

'I'm going to Auntie Glad's. Are you coming?'

'No. I've got homework. Cross the road at the lights and go straight there,' he said automatically. She would, but Mum always told him to look after her. When she was safely out of the house he went upstairs and put his jeans on, stuffing the ink-stained trousers at the bottom of a drawer. He daren't tell Mum what had actually happened. She was a fighter. She'd ring up the school, then Steve Weir's lot would be in for it. It would make matters worse, not better. He could put his old trousers on tomorrow and wait for a good moment to explain. She was so busy with the shop she might not notice.

Back downstairs Worm got out his History file and his felt pens. They were doing a project on Oliver Cromwell. First he had to read all about the Battle of Edgehill, then finish off a picture they'd started in class.

He was rather good at drawing. He'd done an enormous Cavalier stabbing a fat Roundhead to death. He got his rubber out. Before he coloured it in he would make the Roundhead look like Steve Weir. He could give him some nice stringy black hair.

The chapter about the battle was quite exciting. There was a picture in the book of a soldier called Jacob Astley, who had said a famous prayer before the fighting started: 'Oh Lord, Thou knowest how busy I must be this day. If I forget Thee, do not Thou forget me.'

Half an hour later Worm was putting the finishing touches to the Roundhead's liquorice hair. 'Please,' he said aloud, to nobody in particular, 'please give me a chance to do something really great, something that'll make them all shut up and leave me alone.'

'Who's that you're talking to, Peter?' his mother said, coming through from the shop. She bent over him and admired the picture.

'That's good, you'll get an A for that I expect. Who was it you were talking to?'

'I wasn't.'

'You *were*,' Patsy said. 'We heard you.'

'I wasn't talking to *anyone*, and leave me alone, *you*.' He got up and pushed her out of the way.

'*Peter!*' his mother shouted after him. 'We were only—'

But he'd run upstairs to have a few quiet minutes with his chest-expanders. When he thought about that ink-bomb down his trousers, Steve Weir in the playground reading that composition out, and everyone sniggering at him, he felt like crying. If only their Patsy hadn't seen it all.

And now they'd heard him talking to himself. Anyway, it was no good praying for miracles. But the next day, in spite of a very bad start, an amazing thing happened.

He arrived at school early, for two reasons. His old school trousers were in the wash so he'd had to put the new ones on, and he'd slipped off early with Patsy before Mum spotted anything. Then there was Steve Weir and his merry men to cope with. The bullying seemed to go in phases, and they'd got a definite craze for it at the moment. If there was anything planned for today, he might mess it up by arriving first and putting all his stuff out of their thieving grasp. It was Football today, and Art. They'd pinch all his clobber if he gave them half a chance, it was always happening. And last time he'd turned up for games without his kit Mr Gill had given him a detention, 'and no messing'. He didn't listen to anything Worm said any more. That boy had more weak excuses than he'd had cold dinners.

But Worm wasn't the first to arrive. It was a cold morning but sunny and bright, the first really good day after weeks of wet weather. It had brought people to school early. Quite a few were in the playground already, talking together in bunches and kicking balls around. There was nobody near the gate but as he walked in he heard voices over by the old climbing-frame they'd kept for the first years. Everyone went quiet when they saw Worm. There was a definite atmosphere.

He hung back, then an electric bell rang in the school. It was twenty to nine and you could go indoors and sort yourself out for lessons. But no one moved. They were all waiting for him.

Worm's insides were wriggling about in panic. The sunlit yard was like an empty battlefield and an unearthly hush had fallen on it. He began to walk across slowly, on wobbly legs, waiting for the enemy guns.

There was a dark knot of people by the climbing-frame. As he came up it dissolved and separated into figures—the Barretts, Steve Weir, Terence Ackroyd, and Craig Weatherall. The gang was there in force.

Somebody had decorated the rusty metal poles and there was a flapping notice stuck to them too. Worm turned his face away and made for the door into school, but the opening was now blocked. Duggie and Ed Barrett, flanked by the rest of them, stood arm-in-arm and were smiling at him. Dithering, Worm took a step back.

'Have a look then, Worm, fabulous isn't it? We got here early to get it all ready.'

Obediently, Worm looked. The entire contents of his games bag were tied to the network of rusty poles: his striped shirt, his big floppy shorts, his great socks. They'd stuffed them with paper, turning them into a kind of dismembered Guy Fawkes, and everything had been hung upside down. The socks had football boots fastened to them and the weight had stretched them right out. They'd fit a ten-foot right-half now, as long as he had matchstick legs.

People were tittering. 'D'you like the notice, Worm?' a boy called out. 'D'you like what it says?' Worm's eyes crept heavenwards. They had dug up a huge pair of white underpants from somewhere and fastened them to the highest bar. They were enormous, wide enough to fit a Sumo wrestler. The notice pinned to them said in curly letters: ROOM FOR GROWTH. Then he noticed something else. Words had been painted on the wall of the outside lavatories in wobbling white capitals: WORM WAS HERE.

He gulped, and blinked the tears back. It was no good turning the tap on, that was just what they were waiting for. He should step forward coolly and pull the stuff down, perhaps even make a joke, casually, over his shoulder. That's what Frud would have done. (And where was Frud, anyway?)

But he was quaking. The eyes of the bully boys blocking the doorway were boring into him like red-hot drills. 'Worm, Worm, makes you squirm,' someone was chanting. Then Steve Weir broke ranks and came down off the step. Behind him the Barretts closed the gap quickly, in case Worm tried to belt through. Then the whole line stepped forward.

Worm bolted. He was so frightened he felt as if his stomach had dropped out and fallen into the playground. But he wasn't staying there. It was all very well, Frud telling him to stand up to them. How would he like it?

He plunged into the climbing-frame, fought his way through the billowing underpants, and got out on the other side, snatching the notice down as he went. He tore down the brick alley and seconds later had locked himself in one of the boys' lavatories. And there he'd stay till they'd all cleared off.

But the whole gang followed him. He'd hardly slammed the door before fists were hammering on it and Steve Weir was yelling, 'Come on out, Wrigley, and give us that notice back. Took me ages that did. It's my property.'

'Have it, then,' Worm squeaked, and lobbed the crumpled paper ball up, over the top of the door. Then the banging stopped. He could hear taps running and people whispering. He stood with his back to them, his eyes closed, taking deep gulps of air. He was going to be sick, he knew he was. If they didn't leave off he'd either vomit or pass out.

'Worm, Worm, makes you squirm,' came the familiar chorus.

'Give over, can't you,' he shouted. 'You're cracked, you lot, you need your heads examining.'

'Temper, temper,' someone called out. 'Here's something to cool you down, anyway. You'll like this, Worm.' And before he'd cottoned on they'd legged that midget Ackroyd up to the top of the door and he felt cold water being poured down on him.

'That's *it*,' he spluttered as it ran down his neck. 'I'm telling. You can't—'

'Telltale tit, Your mam can't knit, Your dad can't walk, Your brother can't talk...' someone started, and Worm's hand was trembling with the door-bolt when, quite suddenly, everything went dead quiet.

'*Out*,' he heard. 'Everybody *out*. You... you... Get out of here, the lot of you. Now, *go!*' He knew that voice well. It was the high-pitched, rather reedy voice of Mr Egerton, the deputy-head.

Five minutes later Worm was hauled out from his hiding-place and made to stand by the climbing-frame while the teacher delivered a lecture about looking after games equipment in a responsible manner. Steve Weir's lot was nowhere to be seen

25

the school was trooping off to Assembly. All the football gear was lying on the ground in a filthy heap.

'And just remember this, Wrigley, next time anyone starts messing about with your stuff or does anything like this, tell your form master. Tell Mr Robertson. You've got a head on your shoulders, haven't you? *Use it*. We can't have this kind of nonsense going on.'

Tell Mr Robertson. The man was barmy. It was more than Worm's life was worth to go trotting off to El Robbo every time Weir and Co. had a go at him. He wouldn't last five minutes.

Worm and the bully boys were sent straight out again after Assembly. He missed half his Art lesson and they missed Swimming. Two seniors supervised the operation. The Barretts were getting WORM WAS HERE off the wall with scrubbing brushes, and Steve Weir was bad-temperedly sloshing a mop over the lavatory floor. Twice Mr Egerton came out to make sure they were cleaning up properly. The school had to look its best today. A VIP was coming later on.

Worm had been punished too. Justice for all. He'd been late for register and El Robbo had sent him out litter-picking in the playground.

And there was rather a lot of litter. Persons unknown had tipped a couple of dustbins over and Worm had to put everything back. It was just lovely picking up soggy crisp-bags and mouldy half-eaten sandwiches, especially with his bare hands.

4

History was third lesson, before break. As soon as it started Worm realized he'd left his file on the sideboard. He'd been in such a panic to get to school early. The teacher, Mr Stuart, a timid mild-faced little man with a bald head, who couldn't keep order, suddenly lost his temper. He'd already given Craig Weatherall a detention for spitting. Then Worm's hand had gone up.

'Yes, Wrigley?'

'I've left my file at home, sir.'

'You've not done it, have you, Wrigley?'

'I have, sir.'

('Worm, Worm, makes you *squirm*,' had started up from the back already. It took more than a bit of washing-down to squash that lot.)

'*Silence!*' It was an attempt to shout but it came out like a squeak. People giggled. Then Terence Ackroyd leaned forward with some compasses and was sticking them in hard. '*Ouch!*' Worm spluttered before he could stop himself.

'Well, have you or haven't you?'

'I have sir, honestly.' His eyes were watering

27

pain, and he was leaning forward out of range of the compass points. 'I'll go home at break and get it, if you'll let me go out of school.'

'Oh, all right, Wrigley.' Mr Stuart sounded embarrassed. The boy hadn't been lying then. But why was he lolling about like that in his desk, and squealing like a rabbit? He was an idiot.

'You can go home for it, I'll give you my permission. But don't let it happen again. And I want it on my shelf by eleven thirty. You'll have to be quick. The talk starts then.'

In all the miseries of the morning Worm had forgotten about the talk. He didn't want to miss that. Billy Micklethwaite was coming. Everyone knew about Billy, he'd gone to their school years ago, before it went comprehensive. He was their most famous old boy.

He'd been a great all-round athlete, a fine runner, and a champion hurdler, and he'd won a gold medal in the Olympics. Now he was a successful businessman with a chain of sports shops. He went on television and radio quite a lot too, doing sports programmes. Darnley people said he was a bit difficult to handle these days, there were too many go-getters asking him favours because of his name. But all the boys wanted to meet him, including Worm. He'd thought he might pick up a few tips about getting fit for the Darnley Race, even speak to him. If he could pluck up enough courage.

But at break he was late coming back with his file. Mum was out when he got home and he'd forgotten key. He'd had to walk round to Auntie Glad's to row hers.

The talk was in the gym. Worm rushed past it on his way to the staff-room. Billy Micklethwaite had already started, and the children were laughing. He pelted down the classroom block and chucked his file on to Mr Stuart's shelf. Then he made his way back feeling irritated. *He was missing the talk.*

It would be much quicker if he cut across the field. You weren't supposed to, but running back along all those corridors would take so long. The school was like a rabbit warren. And people weren't allowed to run anyway. Someone might see him.

He slipped out of a back entrance, crossed the senior playground, and started to sprint across the field to the gym. Half-way across he stopped and looked back. He thought he had heard a door opening, but there was nobody in sight.

Then Worm smelt something. He hadn't lived behind their shop for nearly three years without learning a few things about cooking fish and chips. Frying things could be dangerous. At the beginning, before Mum had bought the new equipment, they'd nearly had a fire. It was that smell now, overheated fat. If it got too hot everything would burst into flames. And then what?

He looked up. The smell seemed to be coming from the Domestic Science area. One of the upstairs cookery rooms had all its windows open, and smoke was curling out of two of them.

Worm's mouth fell open. The school had a palish green roof. It had started as a very cold morning, but now the sun was high in the sky and it was getting warm. Smoke was everywhere, drifting out of the windows and up through the tiles, thin puffs of grey that floated out and disappeared into the blue sky. And the smell was getting worse.

He panicked. There could be nobody in that room. Everyone was in the gym, listening to Billy Micklethwaite. Some fool must have gone off to the talk and left a pan on, or a whole oven perhaps, and something had caught fire.

Worm knew the school regulations off by heart. They were nailed to a wall near his desk: 'In case of fire SOUND THE ALARM. Close all windows. Do not run. Your nearest exit is: Outside cloakroom in B corridor.'

This was the moment he'd prayed for, the chance to show them all what he was made of, the chance to shine. All he had to do was to set that fire-bell ringing, and he knew exactly where to find it.

He ran inside, tripping up over the concrete steps, and fell flat on his face. Even his shoes were too big, they felt like boats on his feet. But he picked himself up quickly and found B corridor. Soon he was standing in front of the glass disc that covered the alarm-bell. He'd often looked at those things, wondering if they actually worked.

His heart was thumping. It was so horribly quiet everywhere. If only one of the staff would come along, he could show them the roof. They'd deal with it.

But there wasn't time. The man who'd fitted the new fire-extinguishers in the shop had told him that. 'Don't dither around if you think there's a fire somewhere,' he'd told Worm. '*Act.* You may save someone's life.' Hundreds of lives were at stake in Darnley Comprehensive. Your life in his hands. He took a deep breath, raised his fist, and—stopped in mid-air. What if he was wrong? He couldn't actually smell burning, not in here. Worm's insides were rapidly turning to jelly. He ran outside again and had a look at the cookery room roof.

It seemed to be getting worse. It looked now as if the actual slates were smouldering, and there was a lot of smoke. Then he had an idea. He went back across the grass to the gym and ran up to the windows. Everyone's back was turned to him and he could see the tall figure of Billy Micklethwaite waving his arms about, up at the front.

Worm tapped on the glass. He could see Mr Egerton near the back. He'd tell him. But the deputy-head was totally absorbed in Billy's enthralling account of how he'd won his Gold. The man was a big-head, and Arthur Egerton had heard it all before. But you had to admit that he was a marvellous storyteller. The kids were loving it.

Then he was dimly aware of someone dancing about outside. He glanced round rather irritably at the small figure jerking up and down on the other side of the glass. It must be one of those little kids again, from the nursery school next door. They were always getting through the school railings to play on the old climbing-frame. It was bigger than theirs.

Then the child rapped on the window. The teacher stood up. This wouldn't do. Billy Micklethwaite wouldn't like a disturbance in the middle of his act.

He took another look at the figure waving at him from the field. Then he did a double-take. It was *Wrigley*, that boy he'd found hiding in the lavatories.

What was he doing out there, capering about like a lunatic? His mouth was open and he was gibbering.

But Mr Egerton couldn't hear anything through the double-glazing. All he took in were Worm's skinny arms threshing about wildly and the floppy pullover sleeves that had fallen down over his hands. What did he think he was doing?

He marched straight up to the window and pressed his face against the glass. 'If you've anything to say to me, Wrigley, come inside and say it. You've no right to be out there anyway.' Then he sat down again and tried to re-tune to Billy Micklethwaite. 'Little tearaway,' he mumbled to the person in the next seat. 'Told him off this morning. I suppose it's his idea of a joke. Honestly, give him a treat like this and he misses it.'

Worm stared numbly at the pattern on the back of Mr Egerton's pullover. He daren't knock again, and it was miles round to the main gym entrance. If only you could see that roof from here. If they would just stand up...

It's no good, Worm, a voice said inside him. It's up to you this is. *Ring the perishing bell.*

Galvanized, he zoomed back across the playground like a clockwork mouse. He ran inside and back to the fire-alarm on B corridor. It seemed to have grown in the last few minutes, it was like a horrible eye glaring down at him. The look in it said 'feeble', 'idiot', 'pathetic', all the words his tormentors whispered at him as he crept along the corridors.

All right. This was it.

Worm squared his puny shoulders and gave the glass a bit of a kick. Even now he hoped someone

32

would turn up and take over. But nobody did, and behind the glass the monster-eye went on staring at him.

He kicked harder. No response. So he bunched up his fist and hammered on the glass. Still nothing. He must have broken a couple of fingers doing that. He ran outside and looked in the playground for a brick. People were always chucking rubbish over the railings. He found half a good one. That'd do it.

He ran back inside and smashed the brick against the glass. Nothing. Then a whirring, clicking noise. Then...

Every bell in the school was clanging and yammering, and feet went pounding past him and over his head, out into the yard. Feeling faint he went outside himself and saw dozens of children filing out of the gym.

Worm had saved the school.

5

Everyone was outside in five minutes flat. The class teachers were checking names off on their registers and the spare staff patrolled the lines of children, giving out order marks to people who talked. Fire-drills had to be done in complete silence.

The bells went on ringing. Billy Micklethwaite stood with the headmaster, resplendent in his natty striped suit and orange tie, looking at his watch. He was annoyed. He'd rearranged a TV interview on 'Sport North-West' to do this talk.

'Funny time for a fire practice, isn't it, Headmaster?' he said, frostily.

But at that moment the bells were drowned by a series of wailing sirens and everyone started to jig about in excitement. Three fire-engines were hurtling up the road. They screamed to a halt in the playground and a dozen firemen poured out like a lot of black and yellow beetles, helmets shiny in the sun, unrolling hoses and rigging up ladders.

In seconds someone had climbed up to cookery room C. Smoke was still wafting about but slowly, and there was much less of it. It just smelt stale now, like the chip shop on Sundays.

The young fireman poked his head in, then withdrew it, and waggled his spare hand about behind him, feeling for a hose. 'Come on, come on, let's be having it then.'

Suddenly a face popped out above his, a pink, creased, ancient face with an electric fuzz of white hair. A furious face. It was Miss Johnson, the senior cookery teacher.

She looked about a hundred years old. She'd been at the school when it had had twenty-three pupils and occupied a room above a butcher's in Green Street. She had taught Mrs Fothergill, Mr Stuart's two sisters, Mum, and Auntie Glad. She was a terror.

'*Miss Johnson*,' the head called up, rather nervously, 'I'm afraid—'

'Don't poke that thing about in here, please,' she told the fireman. 'We've got problems of our own here this morning.' Then she said very loudly, 'Why wasn't I told about this fire practice, Headmaster?'

(That was the thing about fire-drills at Darnley Comprehensive. You were told in advance. It was daft.)

'Miss Johnson, it is *not* a practice. You must evacuate your room and bring your class with you. At once,' he added feebly.

'*Mr Fothergill*,' came the majestic reply, 'I am in the middle of deep-frying. The girls have important examinations in June. Practicals in a few weeks. They can't be inconvenienced by a silly fire-drill. And, in any case, it is obviously a mistake. *Where is the fire?*'

She slammed the window shut. The little fireman wobbled and nearly fell off his ladder. No fire.

mistake. The whole school sagged visibly and Worm's eyes slid slowly up to the school roof.

The faintest wisps of grey were still drifting off the tiles and up into the brilliant sky. He couldn't understand it. There was no smoke at all now coming out of the cookery room windows, and Miss Johnson was banging them shut, one by one, snorting loudly like an old carthorse. The firemen were coiling their hoses up and staring irritably at the roof, and Mr Egerton was talking to the chief, looking very embarrassed.

The head spun round and faced the school.

'All right. It was a false alarm. I want to know who smashed the glass on B corridor and started all this, and I want to know now.'

Nobody spoke. Teachers and children peered round. Billy Micklethwaite hitched up his knife-edged trousers and fiddled with his tie. Steve Weir picked his nose.

'Very well. If I don't have an answer in one minute the whole school will stay behind at four o'clock for one hour. The half-holiday Mr Micklethwaite had asked for will be cancelled and nobody will take part in next term's Race. And that's just to be going on with. If I don't—'

Then a thrill, rippling along the lines of first years. Worm had stepped forward and was trying to keep his trembling hand in the air.

'It was me, sir.'

Class 1R gasped. Frud looked down through his ~nny glasses at his friend Worm and didn't believe ~he Barrett twins goggled at each other, and ~ring started up all over the place.

'*You? Why?* What's your name? Whose form are you in? How old are you? *Stand up straight when you speak to me!* Come here.'

Worm felt sick. He took a step forward, shaking.

'Peter Wrigley, sir. I'm twelve, sir. I'm in 1R.'

Mr Fothergill looked down. He saw a small, white-faced boy in inky trousers and a grey school sweatshirt several inches too big for him, turned back at the wrist in great bunches. He was very bony. His knobbly wrists lolled out of his shirt sleeves, with long hands stuck on the end. His pale hair looked scanty. Hair like that never lasted. This boy would be bald at twenty.

Wrigley... that name rang a bell. He'd heard that name once already today. Some bullying, wasn't it, some horseplay in the outside cloakroom, and litter all over the playground? Now he was in trouble again. He didn't look as if he had it in him either.

'Wrigley. Weren't you the boy Mr Egerton reported to me this morning? First you disgrace yourself by silly behaviour before school, then you ring the fire-bell. Why, may I ask? Have you taken leave of your senses?'

Worm's throat was raw with fear. He looked round wildly for the deputy-head. He might back him up, he'd seen him outside the gym and not understood. But Arthur Egerton was trying to pacify the chief fire-officer in the staff-room.

The voice that came from his mouth was a hoarse croak. 'I thought I saw smoke, sir.'

'*What?* Speak up, don't mumble. You've got a tongue in your head, I presume, if nothing else.'

'Smoke, sir. I thought it was smoke coming out of

the cookery room roof. There was nobody about and I... I could smell something.'

Some of the children tittered.

'*Silence!* What did you smell, Wrigley?'

'Very hot fat, sir. I thought a pan had caught fire, sir. My mum—'

'I'm not interested in your mum, Wrigley, or in what you thought you might have smelt. Didn't it occur to you to find a member of staff before you got hold of *this* and set all the bells ringing?' He held up the piece of brick that Worm had used to smash the glass.

'I tried, sir. I tried to tell Mr Egerton but—'

But Mr Fothergill swept on. He was in no mood for excuses. In another frame of mind he might have listened to Worm but he was too aware of the tall disapproving figure of Billy Micklethwaite hovering behind him. He had a bunch of car-keys in his hand. He'd be off in a minute. The head was mad. They'd been trying for years to get him to visit Darnley Comprehensive and couldn't believe it when at last he'd said yes. And now this boy had ruined everything.

'In my hand,' he said, waving the brick, 'I have evidence of a very stupid action, the action of a boy who *leapt* before he *looked*, the evidence of a very *stupid* boy. A boy who ruined Mr Micklethwaite's talk, brought three fire-engines out on a false trail, and disrupted an important lesson.'

There was complete silence. Worm's ears sang with nerves. It was as if his scalp was stretching and was about to split open. His cheeks were so hot he felt the tears that filled his eyes might spill over and run

38

down, turning to steam so that everyone would know.

'Well, what have you to say for yourself, Wrigley?'

For a minute Worm couldn't speak. He wanted to say, 'I thought I was doing something important. I thought this was my chance, the one I'd asked for, to do something good, so they'd all stop going on at me. Something brave.' At last he whispered, 'Nothing, sir.'

'Go to my room. Now. Stand outside and wait for me.'

Very slowly, Worm went. When he lifted up his feet it was as if there were two lead lumps on the end of his legs. It was a feeling he'd had only in dreams, when he was terribly frightened and couldn't run away.

It took him hours to cross the playground, and all the time there was silence. Then, just as he reached the door, laughter rippled across the asphalt. They were all laughing at him, even some of the teachers.

The headmaster's desk was covered with papers. Worm's school records were right on top, in the middle. He'd made the boy wait ten minutes before he called him in, so that he could read through them all. It had been a very long wait for Worm.

'What you saw was *steam*, Wrigley,' Mr Fothergill said at last, looking up from his desk.

'Yes, sir.'

'It was cold this morning, there was a frost in the night. When that happens and it warms up later on, the roof-tops *steam*. The sun turns the icy patches to water, then to *steam*. It evaporates. Haven't you ever seen that?'

'No, sir.'

It was all right for Mr Fothergill and people like Pig Baxter, living out at Beeswood on the edge of Darnley, where the moors swept right down to your back garden. All right for people like Frud, who went out with picnics, looking at birds. He'd like to do that too. But where they lived it was row after row of terraced houses. It was all shut in. They only had a yard, and that looked out on to a factory wall, four storeys high.

'Well, it's about time you kept your eyes open a bit more, isn't it, Wrigley? Had a look at what's going on around you. That's the way you learn, isn't it, eh?'

'It looked like smoke to me, sir,' Worm said doggedly. 'And it *was* smoke, coming from the cookery room window.'

'All right, I'll grant you that. But you should have *thought*, Wrigley, used the old brain, eh?' He tapped his own head. 'Made a fool of yourself, haven't you?'

Brilliant, Worm thought.

Mr Fothergill was beginning to feel rather uncomfortable. The boy looked so wretched. His face was chalk-white and his dangling hands shook. He did have a point: it had obviously looked like smoke to him; but Arthur Egerton had thought he was just playing daft outside the window. It was too late now. But he'd have to see the form master about this bullying.

He took refuge in Worm's school report book. Last term's was dismal: 'Maths: Very limited understanding. Geography: Does not seem able to grasp the simplest essentials. French: I know he is alive because I saw him breathe.' That was old Wally Davies. He liked writing reports.

'I've been looking at your marks, Wrigley. Not good, are they? Don't like them. Time you pulled your socks up. *Eh?*'

Worm stared at the floor.

'Look at me, Wrigley, don't slouch. Stand up straight now, shoulders back. Come on.'

Worm looked at him unwillingly, then gave a loud sniff, and rubbed his eyes.

Mr Fothergill shuffled about in embarrassment and stared out of the window. Then he said, quite kindly, 'Look Wrigley, forget about it now. Anyone can make a mistake. We're nearly at the end of term and you've got the Easter holiday to look forward to. I hear you're going youth-hostelling with some friends?'

'Yes, sir.'

'Well, enjoy it. It'll do you good. Lots of fresh air and exercise. You look as if you could do with it. When you come back to school all this will have been forgotten. Right?'

'Yes, sir.'

'You can go then.'

'Thank you, sir.'

It would not be forgotten. His stupidity had been exposed in front of the whole school; all the children, all the staff, and Billy Micklethwaite. After Dad's accident it was the worst thing that had ever happened to Worm. Nothing else could go wrong now, nothing that mattered.

6

Then Frud's brother broke his leg. It wasn't an interesting accident either, like spraining your ankle on a mountain or getting knocked off your skateboard. It was a real Frud-type accident.

Their six-year-old kid brother Gary had left his Lego all over the landing. Graham was as shortsighted as Frud and he was drifting down to breakfast with his nose in a book. (Who but a Hudd would read on the stairs?) He just went *crash*, clattered down the whole flight, and split his shinbone on the last step of all. Ouch. The pain was so bad he fainted, and their Gary got a good hiding.

It meant going youth-hostelling with Pig Baxter in sole charge of them, or simply not going. And Worm didn't like Pig, to put it mildly. Frud had had a hard time persuading him to come on the holiday at all, when he knew who was going with them.

'Look, Worm,' he'd said patiently, 'we can't go unless an older boy goes with us. My parents wouldn't let me, and I bet your mum wouldn't either. You're my friend, he's friendly with our Graham. They won't bother with us much, anyway.

We can do things on our own. Go on, you will come, won't you?'

'Can't understand why your Graham goes round with Pig Baxter.'

The Hudds lived in a semi-detached house in Moorland Avenue, Beeswood, a suburb of Darnley. They had a small neat garden with flower-beds and standard roses, but at the end of their road were the open moors. Also at the end of the road was the Baxters' bungalow. It was huge. It occupied a two-acre plot and had six bedrooms, a dream kitchen, a billiard-room over the garage, and a swimming-pool. The money to build it had come from Baxter's Spring Works which Pig's father had inherited from his uncle, Horace Baxter, said to be the richest man in Darnley, and the meanest.

Pig's parents weren't mean though, you had to admit that. The day after Graham's accident Worm, Mum, and Patsy took a bus up to Moorland Avenue for a last-minute conference about the Lake District trip. Pig's mother, Vi, served an enormous tea from two gold trolleys. The Wrigleys and the Hudds were plied with sandwiches, scones, and three kinds of cake. The children had frothy milk-shakes and Mars Bars. No wonder Pig was fat.

Worm, half-suffocated by soft chintzy cushions on the gigantic settee, watched him eating an éclair. Paul was his real name, but only his parents called him that. Pig suited him better. He had a very smooth, pink face, and small pale eyes with a permanently screwed-up look, as if he had some difficulty seeing out over his bulgy cheeks.

Paul, the Baxters' darling only child, should have

43

been sent away to a posh boarding-school. That's what his dad had wanted, really. But his mother worried about his health. He certainly had plenty of days off. 'Delicate' was the word she used about him. Worm thought he looked about as delicate as an army tank.

'I see no reason at all why the three of you shouldn't go off on your own. Do you, Vi? It'd be silly to cancel all the arrangements now, and I know you'll be sensible and do what Paul suggests.' Dickie Baxter's voice was as smooth as chocolate. He was used to getting people organized.

Worm noticed that he called Mrs Wrigley 'Doris'. He didn't like that, even though Dad had worked for Baxter's. And that was another thing, without Dickie Baxter's help Mum would never have got the shop going.

'Just you remember that, Peter,' she said, when they got back home and Worm was still grumbling about having to go on holiday with Pig Baxter. 'His father's been very good to us.' That was one of the main reasons Worm resented Pig, he was a Baxter and the Baxters had a hold on them. They needed the money the factory sent every month. Pig was the kind of person who might come out with that in public. He was a show-off too: Bighead Baxter, the boy who had everything; he'd been in the crowd laughing at Worm when Steve Weir had read that composition out.

Nobody liked him, really. The only reason Graham put up with him was because the Hudds didn't see the bad in people. So long as they could get on with their nature books and their birdwatching,

44

they wouldn't mind who tagged along with them on holiday, provided they kept quiet at critical moments.

Unlike Worm. He knew exactly who he liked and who he didn't. And he detested Pig Baxter.

Nevertheless, all three of them were on a train two days later, going to the Lake District. They sat in a line. Pig had pushed in first and grabbed the seat by the window. Frud sat at the other end with a big book of glossy photographs spread open on his knees. Pig's dad had given it to them as they boarded the train. Worm was squashed in the middle.

Mum sat opposite, with Patsy and Auntie Glad. They were going to Blackpool for a few days in a boarding-house. It would be the first real holiday Mum had had for three years.

Worm glanced at his mother. She was thinner than she used to be, and she had frown-marks between her eyebrows. She had once looked a lot younger. Now she seemed tired all the time, and a bit depressed. She hadn't really said much about those trousers. It had worried Worm in a way.

Auntie Glad had spoken to him in private. 'Your mum's got to have this week's holiday, Peter, she needs it. If we don't get her out of that shop she'll make herself ill. So you won't let me down, will you, love? If you don't want to go to the Lake District, you can come with us. They'll squeeze you in somehow.'

Worm wanted to cooperate, he liked Auntie Glad. But he couldn't face a week in Blackpool with Patsy. It'd be playing on the sands all morning, then going round the shops after dinner. He'd rather stay in Darnley.

Mum, Patsy and Auntie Glad got off at Preston. Worm stood at the open window and waved them out of sight. He didn't go straight back to the others but stood staring at the rush of houses and gardens as the train gathered speed. He half wished he'd gone with them. He felt lonely now.

Pig had decided to go through the contents of his rucksack, now there was more room. He undid all the straps and spread everything out on the table between the seats.

'Look at these, Worm, aren't they fabulous?'

Worm looked at the new climbing boots, pale leather with chunky laces and 'Made in Italy' stamped on the soles. The smell of them filled the compartment.

'Cost a bomb, these did. My dad said good boots were an absolute *must*. Kills your feet otherwise, when you get higher up and there's hardly any grass.'

'Have you tried them out?' asked Frud.

'No. Well, I walked up our garden in them.'

'They might rub, that's all, and give you blisters. You should really break boots in. I've brought our Graham's old ones.'

'Yes, they look old,' Pig said rudely. 'And I don't need your advice, thank you. You can't buy better boots than these, you know.' Frud could be a bit cheeky sometimes, a bit of a know-all. Just because he was top of his class. Pig was nearly two years older, almost fourteen. He'd better show him who was boss *now*, at the very beginning. He glanced at the old boots swinging gently overhead, tied firmly on to Frud's rucksack with their laces. The leather was creased and spotted, the soles worn. They were boots of character.

Frud said nothing but went on looking at the photographs. Pig decided to have a go at Worm.

'Let's see your boots then, Worm.' His would be falling apart, no doubt. Pig felt superior, he liked new things.

Worm went pink, then mumbled, 'I've not got any.'

'Not *got* any? Not got any *boots*? What are you going to walk in then, you daft nit?'

'Some strong shoes. My school shoes. They'll do, won't they?'

Pig's thick mouth twisted into a sneer. *School shoes.* They wouldn't last five minutes on those mountain tracks. Trust Worm. Surely his mother could have provided something better than that, she got Dad's money every month. And look at his clothes, the cheap yellow kagoule and the patched jeans. Pig didn't like being seen with him, really.

'Why didn't your mother buy you the proper gear, Worm?' he demanded. 'Surely she could have—'

'Leave off, Pig,' Frud said suddenly from his corner. He'd seen Worm's face. It was turning steadily from pale pink to dark red. He'd be crying in a minute. If only he'd stand up to Pig a bit.

'I'm only—'

'Leave off.'

Pig opened his mouth, then shut it. He shrugged and pulled a face at Frud. There was a definite atmosphere in the compartment now.

'Shoes'll be fine,' Frud said to Worm quietly. 'Lots of people walk in shoes. Anyway, the warden at the hostel might have some spare boots you could borrow, you never know.'

47

Pig had started to empty all the pouches on his enormous rucksack. He brought out a complicated compass in a leather case, a camera, a five-bladed pen-knife, a bag of chocolate bars, and several cans of fizzy drink. He decided to be big-hearted. He couldn't start eating and ignore those two, anyway.

'Have a Mars bar,' he said, holding the bag out.

Frud took one. 'No thanks,' Worm said stonily. He was thinking, It might choke me, coming from you.

At the next station two young men got in with rucksacks. They wore kagoules, woolly hats, and stout boots. They smiled at the three young boys, then got books from their packs and started to read. Pig inspected them carefully from his window corner. He might move over to their side in a minute and start talking to them. They were more his class of person. And he'd make it quite clear that he was doing the other two a favour, bringing them on this holiday. Really, they were just kids.

Frud was absorbed in the photographs, Worm was staring glumly out of the window, the men were reading. Pig was *bored*. He was used to being entertained on long journeys, plenty of stops, a lot of sweets, electronic pocket-games to pass the time. He decided to get that book back from Frud; after all, it was his.

'Hang on a minute,' Frud said, 'I'm just reading this bit. This is a fabulous book, Pig, but it weighs a ton. You can't lug it all round the Lakes with you.'

'Oh, I'll post it back home. I've got loads of cash on me.'

'What will we need money for?' Worm said nervously. 'The hostel's been paid for and everything.'

48

His mother had given him a pound or two, but only for emergencies.

'Well, if it rains or something. We'll need money then. To go to the pictures and things.'

'The *pictures*?' spluttered Frud. 'How near do you think they are to a cinema in a place like that?' He jabbed a finger at one of the photographs. Pig looked and his pink cheeks grew pinker. He saw a long, dark lake, the colour of tin, with stony screes hurtling down straight into the water. At the end three mountains reared up jaggedly, their flanks patched with big cloud patterns. A solitary house clung to a fellside and there were blobs below it that looked like sheep.

'Where's that, then?'

'Wastwater.'

'Well, how *do* they get to the pictures from a place like that?'

Pig was used to getting his own way. He didn't give up easily.

'I don't think they go,' said Frud.

7

'Come on you two,' Pig yelled. 'That's our bus. We've only got a minute. Can't you move quicker than that?'

He'd been horrible in the last two hours, self-important, bossy, and very bad-tempered, bellowing instructions at them as they changed trains at Oxenholme, so everyone on the platform turned round and stared. His father had written every detail of their journey down on a piece of paper. He kept losing it and blaming them.

Now he was chivvying them to get a move on as they scurried along the pavement towards the coach stop in Windermere. His gigantic rucksack, with its cargo of chocolate, Coca-Cola, and boots, quite weighed him down. He looked extremely hot.

'Whew!' he snorted as the other two caught up with him. 'Thought you said it always rained in the Lake District. I'm boiling!'

Pig was sly, in spite of all the bluster. He'd managed to get Worm to carry the book of photographs. Frud was cross about that. He looked as his friend shifted it uncomfortably from one arm to the other and willed him to drop it in a puddle, in the middle of the road. But he decided to keep quiet. If Worm really wanted to act as a sherpa for Pig Baxter on his Royal Progress that was his funeral. Pig wouldn't get *him* fetching and carrying.

'Have you seen the name of this bus?' he said, as they found the right stop.

'No.'

'It's called the Lakeland Goat. Look, it's painted on the side.'

It was an ancient single-decker, painted green, with a square bonnet, the kind of bus that would have a smiling face in a children's picture book.

'How old d'you reckon it is?' Worm said doubtfully, looking at its patches of rust as he clambered up after Pig.

'Oh, thirty years old at least,' Frud said.

Pig objected to the shabby bus. All the other tourists were boarding brand-new vehicles, long, streamlined, and gleaming, with proper storage compartments for the luggage. In this thing you had to sit with your stuff on your knee. It was most uncomfortable. And the bus had a funny smell too. It wasn't what he was used to at all.

'Why've they given us this thing?' he complained loudly. 'What's wrong with a bus like that one, over there?'

'Operational difficulties,' Frud said slowly, as if he was talking to a three-year-old. 'There was a notice up, apologizing. Didn't you read it? They must have had a breakdown or something.'

'Trust *us*,' Pig moaned, 'trust us to be landed with something antique. And it stinks too.'

Worm quite liked the old leathery smell. It reminded him of trips to North Wales, years ago, when Dad was alive.

The decrepit bus trundled off through the streets of Windermere. The boys looked out of the window and saw walkers striding along the road, their bulging packs strung about with tin mugs and ice-axes.

'What do they need those for, Frud?' Worm asked.

'Oh, there'll still be ice and snow on one or two of the peaks. Look.'

At the head of the lake Worm saw mountains, range upon range of them. They looked unreal, as if someone had cut them out of paper and stuck them down, one in front of another. Some of the higher ones were capped with snow.

'Glad we're not going up there,' Worm said quietly.

'We are,' Frud said. 'Look at the route. Hope this old bus makes it.'

Worm followed his finger on the map. 'These black arrows show how steep the road is,' Frud explained.

'Will it be as steep as that road over Blackstone Edge?' Worm said fearfully. A creepy feeling was doing strange things to his insides. That was the steepest hill round their way, it went straight up over the moors. Worm hated going over it, he got dizzy. There was one point when he always shut his eyes, the land fell away so steeply down a bank. He felt the bus might skid suddenly and career off the road.

'It'll be much steeper than *that*. Look, Worm, we're

in a mountain region now. That's why we've come. Honestly, you're scared of heights and Pig wants to go to the pictures. You're pathetic.'

It was quite a bold speech for the easy-going Frud. But he was irritated. He'd dropped his *Lakeland Birds Handbook* and he had just spotted something interesting out of the window.

Worm saw the book under a seat. He didn't want to fall out with Frud. If he went off in a mood, leaving Worm to the mercies of Pig Baxter, that'd finish everything. He may as well go home if that happened.

'Here you are, Frud,' he said, squeezing down in front of Pig and rescuing the book.

'Oh, thanks.' He was happy again. He turned to the index, muttering to himself. Pig was investigating a big packet of sandwiches his mother had provided for tea. Honestly, he never stopped eating. No conversation from *them* for the next ten minutes. So Worm looked out of the window.

The bus was labouring up a steep, narrow road with stone walls on each side. The gears made a continuous grinding noise and someone at the back was singing, 'She'll be coming round the mountain when she comes!' The driver had to keep pulling in to the side to avoid cars coming down in the opposite direction, and the walls rushed up to Worm, then fell away violently, making him feel sick. There was a lot of irritable horn-blowing too. It wasn't exactly the peaceful country scene.

Trees in full leaf bordered the road so the views were blotted out. The bus crawled up to the summit of a pass. 'She'll be wearing silk pyjamas when she comes!' bellowed the man at the back as the bus slowed right down and actually started to run backwards.

I wish you'd *belt up*! Worm thought to himself. And I wish this flipping bus would *stop*!

Five minutes later it did. There was a sudden loud hissing noise at the front and the driver rammed his brakes on. Everybody was thrown forward.

'OK. Ten minutes' break here. Engine's a bit hot, nothing to worry about. Everybody out, please.'

They all trooped obediently off the bus. 'This is always happening,' someone was grumbling. 'Even the breakdown relief bus breaks down. It's about time they got rid of this one, it's only fit for the scrapyard.'

Pig was interested in engines. He walked round to the front of the bus and peered into the fizzing radiator. 'We've just bought a new Mercedes,' Worm heard him inform the driver. Typical.

Frud was looking through his binoculars. The man who'd been singing at the back sat down on the grass next to him and glanced at the bird book. 'Not bad,' Worm heard, 'not at all bad. But the best one on the market...' *Bird talk*. The man was tall, skinny, brown, with proper walking breeches and a tweed hat. He looked horribly fit.

Worm turned his back on them and walked away from the bus, looking for a bit of grass that was free from sheep droppings. He sat down miserably. The bus ride had really unnerved him. He didn't think he'd ever get up those mountains, now he'd seen them close to. They were huge. He'd get vertigo and fall off.

He stared out across a lonely valley. They had climbed to the top of a pass between two mountains and were just over the lip of it. Now the road unfolded itself in an endless white zig-zag over browny slopes. A notice on the verge said: VERY STEEP HILL. ONE IN FOUR. ENGAGE LOW GEAR. Worm gulped.

'Here,' Frud said, coming over. 'Have a look through these, you can just see the hostel.'

Worm fiddled with the binoculars till he got a clear picture. He could see a red car going along a road that crossed a valley floor. The fields on each side sloped upwards and became fells, all bumpy and brackeny, feathered with small trees. It looked as if a giant had moulded a few lumps of clay and just dumped them there, in the loneliest place he could find. At the far end was a lake, looking like a flat piece of silver in the sunshine. Above it Worm could see a house, with a flag fluttering on the roof.

'Have you spotted the hostel?'

'Is that it? That place with the flag? But it's in the middle of nowhere!'

'I know. Isn't it great?'

8

Half an hour later the Lakeland Goat rattled up to a farm gate and stopped. 'There you are lads, Easemere Vale Youth Hostel. It's just a step up from here. Mind where you put your feet.'

The three boys got out. The man in the hat handed their rucksacks down, then climbed off the bus himself.

'So long, Bill.' He waved at the driver and the bus clanked off. On the gate was a big green triangle that said YHA and next to it was a hand-painted sign with an arrow: YOUTH HOSTEL TWO MILES UP THIS TRACK.

'What!' Pig exploded. 'I thought we were here. I thought that bus took us right to the door. Two miles' walk, and look at it!'

The path on the other side of the gate was stony and very steep. It wound up from the road and plunged quickly into trees. There was no sign of the hostel, not even the flag. The man from the bus pushed the gate open. 'Coming boys? It's only a hop. See you up there.'

'What's he doing here?' Pig said, scowling. 'Thought this was a *youth* hostel. Look at him, he's ancient, he's years older than my dad.'

'Shh… he'll hear you,' Frud said.

'What do I care? He *is* old.'

'Youth-hostelling's for the young in heart,' Frud murmured in a dreamy voice, looking ahead at the backcloth of distant mountains. 'It's not just for children. I bet he's been coming here for years. He looks very fit anyway. Oh, come on, Pig, what are you doing?'

'Putting my boots on. If it's a two-mile walk I may as well try them out.'

Rather unwillingly Frud sat down on the grass and Worm got down beside him. Then he had a thought. While Pig's back was turned, and with Frud looking on and grinning, he opened up the mouth of Pig's rucksack and wedged the big book inside.

Pig noticed immediately. 'Oh, come on, Worm,' he bossed. 'Give us a break, will you? My pack's twice as big as yours. I can't carry that book as well as everything else.'

Whose fault's that? Worm was thinking. You stuffed all that food in it. Pig's a good name for you.

But he just said, 'Sorry, Pig, but my arms are aching, honestly.' Then he ran after Frud.

'Typical,' he heard. 'That's just like you, Worm. Ungrateful's not in it. That's what you are, *ungrateful*.'

'That's it,' Worm thought bitterly. 'I knew he'd get round to it sooner or later, our family and his dad's money. It's started.'

They began tramping up the path in earnest. The man was yards ahead already, walking effortlessly, swinging a stick. He made the bulging pack on his back look as light as a feather.

He's a professional, Worm thought enviously, he knows what he's doing. I'm going to watch him. The chest-expanders were at the bottom of his rucksack. He hoped there'd be somewhere quiet where he could do his exercises in the mornings. He hadn't missed a day yet, and he was sure his biceps were toughening up already.

He suddenly felt more cheerful, in spite of Pig. The path wasn't too bad and he was keeping up with Frud quite easily. His friend plodded along silently, his long legs set in a steady loping rhythm. He was bound to be a good walker after all those rambles with his dad and their Graham.

After about a mile they came out of the trees and got a view of Easemere Lake. The water glinted in the afternoon sun and two birds winged over it, calling to one another.

'Can't we stop?' Pig called from the back. 'My feet really hurt.'

'Oh, come on,' Frud shouted back. 'We've stopped twice already. We're nearly there now.'

'*Look*,' Pig said, puffing up to them, 'I'm in charge and I want a breather. It's all right for you two, you've not got this lot to carry. These boots are rubbing me. I'm getting blisters.'

'If you just keep on going you'll get your second wind,' Frud said patiently.

'But it's so *steep*.'

'Oh, stop moaning,' Worm said under his breath.

But Pig heard. He made an almighty effort, ran forward clumsily in the stiff boots, and grabbed Worm by the shoulder, digging his nails in hard. 'Listen you,' he began angrily, 'I heard that. Who do you think you are? Say that again and I'll thump you. If it wasn't for me you wouldn't be here, *see*?' and he tightened his grasp through Worm's thin yellow kagoule.

Worm wanted to say, 'Wish I *wasn't* here. Wish I was sitting on Blackpool sands with me Auntie Glad.' Instead he whispered, 'Sorry, Pig.'

Frud stood in the middle of the path with his arms folded, looking from one to the other. He didn't know what to do. Worm would be better off if he didn't say 'sorry' all the time. Perhaps he was right though, for once in his life, saying they shouldn't have come with Pig Baxter. But if he sided with Worm openly he might come off worse in the end. Pig was sneaky. His brother had warned him about that. He might start getting at Worm when Frud wasn't there.

Perhaps they could shake him off when they'd settled in at the hostel. If there were older boys Pig would probably try to pal up with them. He seemed embarrassed at being seen with Frud and Worm.

'Come on,' he said evenly. 'If we get a move on we'll be first inside when they open the doors. We can bag the best bunks. The shop may be open too, they sell sweets and things, but they'll only have a limited supply out here.'

Pig moved into first place, at the head of the party, and actually quickened his pace.

The youth hostel stood in a field cropped close by sheep. It was a low wooden building, rather like a Swiss chalet, with large windows overlooking the lake. The front door was locked. Outside a blackboard said: OPEN 5 P.M. ALL BEDS BOOKED TONIGHT.

'It's only a smallish hostel,' Frud explained. 'Some are enormous. Good job we booked in advance. This one always fills up quickly, it's so close to the fells.'

'Yes,' Worm said, glancing behind him. From the back door of the hostel you stepped straight out on to a mountainside. A track wound up into the foothills of a whole range of peaks. In the clear light the summits looked close, as if you could touch them.

'They're quite near, aren't they?' he said.

'Oh, no, not really. A good nine miles the closest one is—well, to the top and back.'

They were all thirsty. Worm walked over to a stream that flowed through the hostel grounds into the lake and climbed over some rocks. Where the water spurted out, over a rocky shelf, he cupped his hands and drank. It was so cold he shivered.

'Nothing like it, is there?' a voice said behind him. It was the man in the hat.

'It's a bit cold, but I like the taste,' Worm said, having another drink.

'There'll be a dead sheep lying in it higher up,' Pig said, pulling the top off a can of Coke. 'You won't catch me drinking that.'

'Oh, push off,' Worm muttered, as Pig walked towards the hostel, swigging from the can as he went.

Pig Baxter was not pleased. What he could see of the hostel, by peering nosily through the windows, didn't look at all promising. It wasn't exactly a five-star hotel. There appeared to be acres of shiny wooden floor, hard chairs, and plastic-topped tables. No carpets to speak of, no comfy settees, no television. Everything looked very basic and extremely uncomfortable. No television! What on earth were they going to do in the evenings? It was miles from civilization. It was a real dump.

He wandered back to the stream and tried to barge in on Worm's conversation with the man in the hat. 'I say, Worm, I don't fancy this place very much. Have you seen what it's like inside?'

But the man appeared not to have heard. 'You just don't realize how much noise there is in a town,' he was saying. 'Did you say you lived in Darnley? Well, you know what I mean then. Oh, I've been to Darnley, we've got friends there. Out here it's different, it's like another world. You can really hear things in a spot like this. I think—'

Then a loud noise shattered everything. Worm saw something white flashing in and out of the trees and heard a car of some kind being driven very badly in low gear. The driver kept sounding the horn and the sheep ran off in fright.

Then he heard, 'All right, we've arrived. Now out you get everybody and don't leave anything behind.'

They heard The Voice before they saw anything. It was a loud female voice, powerful enough to shatter glass, a trumpeting, commanding voice. Then they saw a white minibus with ST HILDA'S SCHOOL painted on the side in blue. Fourteen girls climbed out of it, brushing themselves down, looking round at each other and tittering.

'Dorothy Marsden, don't drop *litter*!' The bellowing voice ripped open the peaceful afternoon and some birds flew up off the lake in a terrified clatter of wings.

'All right, Gert, all right,' someone said quite loudly, a tall girl of about Pig's age, with frizzy orange hair and high-heeled shoes. 'Keep your hair on.'

61

The woman Gert smiled blandly at Worm, Pig and Frud, and at the man in the hat, as they all stood to attention by the tumbling stream.

'Marvellous spot, isn't it? Here to do some walking, are you? Good-o, so are we.'

Oh, no, groaned Worm to himself.

Pig said aloud, 'When's the next bus back?'

9

'All right, folks,' said a cheery voice. 'Who's my first customer?' A small stocky man with curly brown hair and a neat moustache had opened the front door.

'I'm Derek Giles, the hostel warden. Now, where've you all come from? I'll need your membership cards first, then I'll tell you which dormitory you're sleeping in. If you've not got a sheet sleeping-bag you can hire one. Now then—'

He was fast and efficient, used to dealing with parties of lively school children. So was the woman Gert. By the time Pig had found their cards and the receipt for the money they'd sent in advance, she was standing foursquare at the counter where the warden had his office and shop, with all the girls lined up behind her in an orderly queue.

Worm studied her massive behind, her solid legs, and her great feet, her heavy walking shoes polished to a high gloss. She wasn't really fat, just solid. All muscle. She looked as if she'd been swinging up mountains since she took her first tottering steps.

'Pleased to meet you,' she boomed. 'I'm Miss Pringle, Eleanor *G.* Pringle. I've brought the party from St Hilda's School.'

Two girls at the back of the queue giggled. 'Listen to that,' one of them whispered, 'Eleanor *G*. I told you it was Gertrude.'

'It's *not*,' the other said emphatically. 'It's Eleanor *Grace*. I saw it written in her school hymn-book.'

'Well, I like Gert better,' the first girl said, addressing Worm. 'We've always called her Gert. Oh, she is awful though.'

'What's your name, then?' asked Worm.

'I'm Millicent Wilkinson and this is my friend, Dot Marsden.'

Millicent Wilkinson was very plump. The way she scraped her straw-coloured hair back into a tight pony-tail made her round face look like a little pink balloon. But she had a very hard stare, the kind of stare clever people have, people who weigh you up. Frud had it.

'Have you been youth-hostelling before?' Worm said, looking down at Dot's high-heeled shoes. She didn't look much like a walker, and neither did Millicent. She must be at least a stone overweight.

'No,' Dot replied. 'And we wouldn't be here now, if it wasn't for Gert.'

'What do you mean?'

'Two people dropped out last week, and Gert said, "Right, two vacancies. I want two volunteers, you and you." Didn't she Mill?'

'Well, not quite. She just said it would do us good, get us fit, and why didn't we think about it. Then my mum was talked into it at the Parents' Evening. Dad said I could go, just as long as I brought my trombone.'

'Your *trombone*?'

'Yes, he conducts a brass band. I've only just started learning, but when you first begin you have to blow it every day. It's here.'

She nudged a peculiar-shaped case with her foot.

A trombone, Worm thought, *and* the woman Gert. It was going to be bedlam.

'Anyway, who are you?'

Before Worm could open his mouth Pig leaned right across him. 'I'm Paul Baxter and these two younger ones are with me. I'm in charge of them. This one's Frank Hudd and—'

'And I'm Peter Wrigley.'

'And he's Worm.'

'Call me Frud,' Frud said quietly. 'Everyone else does.'

But Millicent Wilkinson wasn't listening. She had fixed Pig Baxter with her hard, clever look. He was the bossy kind of individual she didn't much care for. She certainly didn't approve of the way he'd elbowed the two others to one side. The dark serious one with glasses didn't seem too bothered by it, but the little thin one looked utterly miserable.

She glanced at him. Everything he had on was a bit too big and they were rather cheap clothes. The fat boy obviously came from a wealthy family. He had a beautiful orange Swedish kagoule, a new rucksack, and very expensive walking boots. He thought a lot of himself. He was going to enjoy patronizing the little weedy one with hardly any hair. Millicent detested him on sight.

'Worm,' he was repeating. 'We've always called him that.'

'*Worm?*' she said. 'Did you say *Worm?* What a ridiculous name.'

'Have you heard this one?' Pig was saying to anyone who would listen:

> *Today I've seen a little worm,*
> *Crawling on his belly.*
> *I think he'd like to come inside*
> *And see what's on the telly.'*

'Very funny,' Millicent said flatly. 'What did you say that boy's name was, Peter? *Pig?*'

Supper was served at seven o'clock: soup, stew and apple crumble. Pig complained that it wasn't cooked properly and that he didn't like custard. There was water to drink, or tea out of a huge urn. Pig wanted pop. Everything seemed all right to Worm. Mum was so busy in the shop at supper-time that a three-course dinner was a luxury to him.

The man with the hat sat at their table. He was called Brian Blake. He told them that he came to Easemere every year at Easter to do some walking. He lived in Oldham with his wife and two grown-up sons. The wife usually came with him but her mother had fallen ill, so she'd stayed behind this year to look after her.

Brian Blake was an Eater. Worm watched him chew his way through four pieces of bread while he ate his soup, and the minute the warden shouted, 'Anyone for seconds?' he was at the hatch before anybody else had moved. Now Worm understood why he'd insisted on sitting at the kitchen-end of their table. It gave immediate access to the grub.

He was a bit puzzled by Brian Blake. He was very friendly but there was something mysterious about him even so. It *was* odd for him to be youth-hostelling all on his own, chomping away in the middle of hordes of school children. He didn't want to enter into proper conversation with anyone either, and he had a precise, rather clipped way of talking, as if he wanted you to know just so much about him and no more. Worm didn't like to admit it but he did wonder if Brian Blake had told them the truth. Why *was* he there?

Frud might have a few ideas. He'd ask him, if they could get away from Pig. If Pig was consulted he'd walk straight up to the man and say belligerently, 'Isn't it a bit funny, you staying in a place like this? Aren't you a bit old?' It'd be just like him.

The food was very plain but there was plenty of it and second helpings for anyone who went up to the hatch. Millicent was almost as big an eater as Brian Blake. 'This food's awfully fattening,' she confided to Worm, tucking into the apple crumble. 'Mum gives me salads all the time at home. I'm turning into a rabbit.'

'You can't be on a calorie-controlled diet *this* week, Millicent,' Gert shouted across from the next table. Then Brian Blake interrupted, 'And, of course, you couldn't eat meals like this all the time, then just sit round all day. You've got to burn it off, by walking. If you didn't you'd soon put weight on.'

'How many miles do you walk in a day?' Frud asked. 'I bet it's a lot.'

'Oh, twelve to fifteen. I'm doing three peaks

tomorrow. Fancy coming with me?' He grinned.

'Well, not *tomorrow*,' Pig said firmly, before the two others could say anything. He was in charge, and he had no intention of walking fifteen miles anywhere, now or ever. The man must be some kind of lunatic.

'Come on, you two,' he said to Frud and Worm, as soon as the meal was over. 'Let's go outside for a bit.'

'Right!' Derek Giles shouted from the hatch. 'Jobs! Miss Pringle, I'd like you and some of the girls to cut sandwiches for tomorrow's packed lunches. Mr Blake, will you sweep the dining-room please? The three boys from Darnley, you're on washing-up. The rest of the girls can help you.'

'Washing-up?' Pig spluttered. 'For all this lot? With no *dishwasher*? He must be having us on.'

'Come on, Pig,' Dot said cheerfully, waving a dish-cloth at him. 'On your bike. It might slim your arms.'

10

Worm woke next morning to the sound of a trombone. He climbed out of his bunk and stood up. The dormitory was empty and through the window he could see Pig and Frud, already up and dressed and sitting by the stream.

He crept along the corridor and peeped into the girls' room. Millicent was perched on a top bunk blowing furiously. Dot sat below her, calmly filing her nails.

'How does it sound?' Millicent shouted down.

'Like an elephant being strangled. What on earth's it called?'

Millicent consulted her music. 'Er… "Folk Song"… No, no, "Frolic". It's called "Frolic".' She put the trombone to her lips and began again.

Dot looked up and saw Worm hovering in the doorway. She smiled at him. 'Oh, hello Peter. What do you think?'

He hesitated. 'It doesn't sound too bad.'

'Oh come on, give us the truth. She says it's called "Frolic".'

Worm listened again. 'Well,' he said slowly, 'it's, er, a little bit flat, perhaps.'

'I think it sounds like a duck in pain.'

Millicent dismantled the trombone, put it in the case, and banged the lid down. 'Oh Dot, you are awful.'

'Why can't you go and sit in a field, and play it there?'

'The warden said no musical instruments or radios were to be played in the evening. *He* suggested before breakfast. Anyway, I promised my dad.'

'Thinks you're going to be Young Musician of the Year, does he?'

'Oh you are terrible.'

By ten o'clock the youth hostel was empty. Miss Pringle and the girls from St Hilda's were making their way slowly along the lakeside before climbing up on to Easemere Crags. This was a small huddle of grassy, low rocks at the end of the lake, with a clear path to the top.

'Just a stroll, girls,' Worm heard. 'About five miles. It will break us in gently.'

'But Miss Pringle, it's *raining*,' Dot moaned, as they all trooped off towards the lake.

'Well you aren't made of sugar, are you, dear? You won't dissolve. If it rains, dear, we'll all get wet.'

Brian Blake had set off much earlier, as soon as the washing-up was finished. Worm had been keeping an eye on him. As the three boys reached the farm gate they saw him striding rapidly along a fell path, his red kagoule a bright splash against the brown.

'Funny,' Frud said, 'he's going in the wrong direction. Thought he was going to climb up the Easemere Pikes today, that's what he told me. He's walking our way, up that valley. It's a dead end.'

A police car had pulled up at the hostel gate and inside Derek Giles was talking to a uniformed officer. They had a map spread out over their knees. The three boys stared at them.

'Come on,' Pig said bossily. 'It can't be anything to do with us. Which path do we take, Frud?'

They'd only gone about ten yards when Derek Giles unwound his window and shouted, 'Hey, you three, can you come here a minute?'

It was raining quite heavily. 'I think you'd better get in,' the policeman said. 'That's it. Got enough room, have you?'

Pig was almost sitting on Worm.

'Get off, will you, I can't breathe.'

'You're not giving me enough room, I can't move over any more. Shove up yourself.'

Worm felt frightened suddenly. Something must be wrong in Blackpool, and they'd come to tell him. It was a policeman who'd come to inform his mother about Dad's crash, three years ago. Worm had opened the door to him. He'd remember that moment as long as he lived.

'These are the boys,' the warden was saying. 'And this one—Frank, isn't it?—knows as much about birds as I do. We had a good old chin-wag last night.'

Frud had spent ages talking to Derek Giles after supper. They'd compared binoculars and discussed bird books. He'd told the warden all about their Rambling Club and listened to a lot of funny stories about running a youth hostel.

'There's nothing that man doesn't know about the wildlife in this area,' he'd told the other two enthusiastically.

'Well, what else is there?' Pig had grumbled, thinking nostalgically about the cinema he'd noticed in Windermere, where they were showing old horror films. He'd seen *Invasion of the Body Snatchers* twice already, on television, but watching that again would be better than tramping round here in a downpour, going up mountains you couldn't see for mist. Youth hostels were pretty spartan, Pig had decided. He didn't like the food or the jobs, and the other boys were much older than he was, so he couldn't really pal up with them. He felt extremely bad-tempered and, most of all, *bored*.

'We've got problems in this valley at the moment,' the policeman explained. 'We just wondered if you could help us.'

The boys sat up and listened.

'Yes, we think we've got egg-stealers. We received a report last night that they're moving into the area. We just wondered if you could keep your eyes open for us, and report anything suspicious.'

'Egg-stealers?' repeated Pig. 'Is that all?' What a let-down. He'd imagined a nasty murder, or a big robbery at the very least.

'Why doesn't the farmer just—'

'Not hens' eggs, *birds'* eggs, you nit,' Frud said impatiently. 'It's the nesting season. It's spring. Or hadn't you noticed?'

Pig felt humiliated. His stupid remark had exposed his ignorance to the warden and the policeman. He wasn't used to feeling small. He said huffily, 'But surely you don't have time to get involved with a few birds' eggs, I mean, with all your other duties?' That sounded better.

'It's a crime,' Frud said solemnly. 'Stealing rare birds' eggs is a crime, because of what it leads to. That's the way a species becomes extinct.'

'But why do people steal them?'

'To put into their own collections, or to sell. Sometimes the people who take them aren't interested in birds at all, they just want to make money out of them. You can get quite a lot for really rare eggs, and even more for chicks. Some people take the young birds from the nest and rear them secretly. Then they sell them. You can get hundreds of pounds for a chick, and they could put you in jail if they caught you. I'm sure that's the law.'

'You're absolutely right, Frud,' the warden said from the front. He and the policeman exchanged pleased looks. This lad knew exactly what he was talking about. They'd been right to let the boys in on the problem.

'Anyway,' the warden went on, 'if you see anything going on that looks the least bit odd, will you come and tell me?'

'What kind of birds are we looking for?' Pig wanted to know. He was using his loud, official voice now. This might get quite interesting, tracking down egg-thieves. A spot of detective-work would certainly liven things up, and there might be some money in it too. His little eyes gleamed. That'd be something to tell Dad about, helping the police. They might get a reward. And the authorities would rely on him obviously, since he was the older one. Nobody could take Peter Wrigley seriously, he was so wet, and Frud was only twelve, for all his brains.

Derek Giles didn't answer. Pig repeated the

question. 'Well, what *are* we looking for? Does anyone else know?' He didn't want anyone else muscling in on the act if this turned into something big.

The warden looked at the officer, then said, 'Let's just say it's a protected species, shall we? I think that's all you need to know. And do keep quiet about it, won't you? Eyes open and mouths shut. See you tonight then. Hope it doesn't rain all day.'

11

Two hours later Pig said, 'That's it. I'm in charge and we're having our lunch; I'm not going another step.'

Frud looked at his watch. 'OK,' he said, 'I suppose we can stop. It's nearly one o'clock. But if we go down as slowly as we've come up we'll still be out here at midnight. You've got to move your feet a bit, Paul, like Worm.'

Worm undid his packet of sandwiches and felt pleased. The person really in charge was Frud, even though Pig was the older one. His idea of being the leader was to be as bossy as possible. He was always arguing with them about the route, and telling Worm where to put his feet, though he obviously hadn't got a clue about walking. All he was interested in was his blisters.

'Save your breath,' Frud kept telling him. 'If you talked a bit less we might get on faster.'

This was a new Frud. He was always so quiet at school. Out here he was tougher, it was as if the wild, bare landscape had somehow got inside him, and was taking over.

Worm looked at him nibbling a hard-boiled egg,

his dark floppy hair blowing about in the wind, his long legs tucked under his chin, his calm, serious face staring out across the fells.

'They've been a bit mingy with the corned beef in these,' Pig said, inspecting his sandwiches. 'I bet that Miss Pringle made mine. And I don't like oranges, either.'

'You might be glad of that orange when we're still walking back at ten o'clock tonight, in pitch darkness,' Frud grunted. He'd had enough of Pig for one day.

Worm looked over his shoulder at the *Lakeland Birds Handbook*.

'D'you know which bird the warden was on about?'
'I think so. It's this one, almost bound to be.'
Worm read:

Peregrine Falcon *Nests in bare scrape on rock ledges in mountain regions, also on sea-cliffs. Lays in April, three to four eggs. Feeding: birds killed on the wing, rabbits, and other small mammals. Remarkable for its breathtaking 'stoop'. Speeds of 180 miles an hour have been claimed for it when diving to locate its prey. The bird's talons may strike with such shattering force that the victim's head is sometimes broken off.*

There was a painting of the bird on the page opposite. It looked cruel. Worm stared at the hooked beak and curved talons with new understanding, trying to imagine something dropping out of the sky at 180 miles an hour and blasting his head off.

Pig came over and studied the disapproving bird carefully.

'Ugh, is *that* what we're looking for? It looks like that woman at the hostel, the one with those girls. What do they call her—Gert?'

Frud shut the book angrily. 'Come on, Worm, let's see if we can find anything up there.' He set off, walking quickly, with Worm behind him.

'Hey, wait for me, can't you?' Pig shouted. 'It was only a joke. Hang on.' Then, when they didn't wait, he got angry. 'Look, you two,' he hollered, 'I'm supposed to be leading, not you. If it wasn't for me—' But he was talking to himself. Frud had already disappeared from sight and Worm, trembling at his own daring disobedience, had clambered up the fell after him, leaving Pig to boss a few sheep around.

They had spent the morning walking up a narrow valley. After a hard scramble at the beginning the track had flattened out. Then it was just a steady walk, first by the side of a stream, then out across the fellside to join a path that went round the valley head in a kind of horseshoe.

'Seen anything interesting yet?' Worm called to Frud as they pulled up a rocky path that led out of the valley.

'No, but I think it's worth going on a bit, now we've got this far. The track seems to peter out just here though.'

Pig laboured up after them crossly. 'Thought we'd reached the furthest point. This isn't a path. What have we come up here for?'

'I'm sure there's a kind of inner valley somewhere,' Frud said. 'My dad brought us once. There's no proper track, I do remember that.'

'Well, in that case—'

'Oh shut up, will you. We won't see anything if you don't keep your voice down.'

They toiled up the rocks for a good ten minutes. Worm was sweating but the wind whistled past him, cooling him down nicely. He was quite enjoying himself. Now he was actually on the mountain, with his face thrust right up against the grass and stones, only able to look a few steps ahead, his nerves had gone. He simply hadn't thought about how high they were.

He stopped and looked back at the long green valley floor blotched with sheep, the small trees clustered along the beck, the great mountains humped over everything so peacefully. He wished Mum could see it all. She'd love this.

From the top the three boys looked down into an almost perfect oval of green. The tiny upper vale was completely ringed with jagged rocks, too high even for sheep. At the far end was a tarn, blue-black like a smooth pebble.

'There'll probably be a stream running into that,' Frud told Pig. 'Let's go down. You keep going on about feeling thirsty.'

'Well, how far is it?'

'Oh, we should get there in about ten minutes. Come on.'

He had gone all quiet and brooding, like milk just before it comes up to the boil. He kept looking through his binoculars and scowling.

'Have you spotted something?' Worm asked.

'Seen one of those birds, have you? There are enough rocks for them here, surely?' Pig said.

'No, no such luck,' Frud muttered, 'but I think there's a tent.'

They found a tiny stream gushing over the rocks and tumbling down into the dark water. Pig filled his empty Coke tin and took a noisy swig. 'Ugh! It tastes foul!'

'You'll survive,' Frud said, running his eyes over the little orange tent.

The entrance was zipped down and securely fastened. The grass round it was bare, but they saw a black circle by some boulders where someone had made a fire.

'It seems a funny place to camp,' Worm said. 'Wouldn't like to be here on my own, would you, or at night? It's so high up.'

The sun was shining now but it was windy. All three had put their kagoules back on over their sweaters. The wind was biting, turning Pig's pink legs all pimply.

'You don't suppose—' he began.

'I don't know. It's just possible...' Frud was saying, looking round at the rocks that hemmed them in. 'You'd only camp in a spot like this if you were doing a really long climb. But all the main peaks are over there; this is miles away from them.'

'Why don't we have a look inside the tent?' Pig suggested. 'Come on, I'm going to.'

But when they actually got to the zipped-up doorway something stopped them in their tracks. Nobody moved, not even Pig.

'I don't think we should,' Worm said nervously. 'They're probably just campers, anyway. There might be someone *in* there.'

'Couldn't be,' Pig said scornfully. 'They'd have heard us by now and come out.'

This was true. Frud crept right up to the tent and put his hand on the zip. 'Hello!' he shouted. 'Hello!'

His voice rang out and the rocky walls turned his firm call to a thinned-out metallic whisper, 'Hello! Hello!' Worm shivered inside. Half of him wanted to run down the valley to the safety of the youth hostel, half of him wanted to stay here, in this bleak wilderness. He'd never in his life been in such a desolate place. As Frud jerked the zip up and peered into the tent fear washed over Worm, making him even colder.

'It's all right. There's no one here.'

'Anything suspicious, though?' Pig said hopefully. Now he'd got his breath back he felt better-tempered. He shoved his way past Frud and went into the tent. If there was anything the police should know about he must be the one to find it.

'D'you think we ought to go right in?' Worm whimpered anxiously from the back. 'I mean, we don't know...' But Frud had gone in too.

'There's nothing unusual in here,' Pig was saying. 'This is only what anyone would bring, if they went camping. Nice sleeping-bags, real down. Pricey these are. My dad was going to buy me one, till you said we had to use those awful sheet things.'

Frud was looking at a map which was spread out over one of the camp-beds. 'Mm... wonder what all those red marks are for? This is a new kind of walking map. It's on a very big scale.'

He knelt down and squinted at it while Pig examined a stack of food packets in a corner and took the lids off some plastic containers.

'Look at all this food. They've brought plenty of

supplies anyhow. Doesn't look as if they intend to move off in a hurry.'

Worm stood dithering in the doorway, peering in. Then he noticed something sticking out from under one of the beds. 'What's that, d'you think?'

Frud looked down, then pulled. It was a flattish box of polished wood with brass hinges and a small lock. He whistled.

'Well, well, well. Clever old Worm. We're in luck.'

'What is it?'

'Ever seen one of these before?'

'No. Is it a tool-box?'

'Use your loaf, Worm. It's for egg-collecting.'

But the box was locked.

'Fancy locking up a flimsy thing like that,' Pig said, disappointed. 'I mean you could just smash it open.'

'And smash what's inside, I suppose?' Frud replied irritably, looking at the lock in frustration.

'Well, I think we should take it to Derek Giles,' Pig said. 'Come on.'

'It's stealing,' Worm started, but Pig pushed at him, trying to get past.

'All right, all right, I'm going,' and Worm turned and stepped outside, right into the arms of a tall, thick-set, bearded man of about twenty, whose bristly hands came down upon his shoulders like iron clamps.

12

It was hard to say who was more surprised, but the man spoke first.

'What on earth do you think you're doing?' he shouted at Worm, and he raised a fist in the boy's face. 'I've got a good way of dealing with people like you. Want a demonstration?' As he scowled down at the terrified Worm, Pig came out of the tent with the egg-box under his arm. A second later Frud's bespectacled face popped through the flap too.

'Give me that, will you!' a second voice commanded, and a fat arm shot out to grab the box. This man was short and stocky. He had a pale, rather pudgy face and small eyes, narrowed down to stare at the three boys who stood limply on the grass outside the tent. Both men wore jeans and kagoules, and both had walking boots.

Somehow though they didn't really look like walkers, in spite of their boots and all the gear in the tent. Everything about them was a bit too new, and they were both rather white-faced. They looked more like indoor types. The shorter one was definitely plump. Regular walking would have got rid of that spare fat, surely, Frud decided. Worm was thinking much the same and silently comparing these two with someone like Brian Blake, with his tanned, lean face and his ancient cord breeches. Pig didn't take to them either. They were much too unfriendly for his liking. Something was wrong. They all felt it.

'What the hell are you doing with our things?' the pudgy one said loudly. 'Clear off or you'll feel this boot in your backside. I'll go for the police if you don't hop it.'

It was a rather ridiculous threat. They were three miles from the proper footpath and hours away from the nearest road. Anyway, he looked so unfit. They'd easily outrun him.

But Worm was frightened. They *had* interfered with the tent, that was trespassing, and Pig *had* been holding the box. The men might lose their tempers and give them all a good hiding. Nobody would know, out here.

'I'm sorry,' Frud began uncertainly. 'We thought we—'

'Look, we're staying at the youth hostel in Easemere,' Pig interrupted, giving Frud a dirty look that plainly said, Shut up and let me talk to them. 'These two young boys are with me. Now last night the police came round and told us that there were people in this valley stealing wild birds' eggs, and we've been keeping our eyes skinned, naturally. We ate our sandwiches by your tent and we noticed it was all undone. That box was lying on the ground. Well, obviously, someone had been snooping around, so we thought we'd better wait till you came back. Have you seen anything, by any chance? If you have, you really should tell the police. You could phone from the youth hostel.'

Worm was staggered to hear all the lies come rolling out. He'd forgotten that Pig was the son and heir of smooth-tongued Dickie Baxter.

There was silence for a minute, and the men looked at one another.

'Huh, well, yes. I see.' The hands on Worm's shoulders relaxed slightly. 'That's a bit different. Sorry, only naturally we thought you'd been going through our stuff. We're, er, on an Outward Bound course, aren't we, Trev? Rest of the lads are down in Wasdale.'

He wasn't such a good liar as Pig. He'd gone very red and he was fumbling for the right words, and shifting from one foot to the other. Anyone would be nervous with Frud staring at him. That cool, clever look so clearly said, Oh yes? Now pull the other one.

Pudgy Trev blustered. 'Well, yeah, that's it. We're up here for a week, survival course like. We meet up with the rest of them on Saturday. We've got to stay here for three days, y'see.'

'Noticed anything suspicious?' Pig threw in slyly. He was cunning. The three boys watched as the bearded one pulled his mouth about and stared at the ground. 'No,' he said finally, 'no, we've not. But we'll certainly keep a look-out from now on. Er, look, do you three want a drink? I'm going to brew up. I'm parched.'

'No thank you,' Pig said, very politely. 'We've got to make a move now, or we won't get any supper. Come on, you two.'

Quickly they gathered their things together,

zipped up their kagoules, and set off. The two men watched silently, side by side in front of the tent. Then the bearded one muttered something to his friend, tightened up his bootlaces, and set off after them. Pig heard him crunching up the stones and stopped dead in his tracks.

'Just seeing you off the premises,' the man called up, in a kind of snarl. It was as if he'd had second thoughts about Pig and Co.

The boys quickened their pace and at last dropped down off the sharp rocks, on the other side of the little valley. The Bearded Wonder was out of sight now, but Pig knew he couldn't have gone back to Pudge, they'd have heard his boots on the scree-covered slopes. Silently he beckoned the others over and made them sit down.

'Now what's up?' Frud said irritably. 'We're losing the light, you know. If it's your boots again—'

'*Shut up,*' Pig whispered and actually put his hand over Frud's mouth. 'You'll see in a sec. This is too good a chance to miss.' He got his camera out of his rucksack and fitted a great black lens on to it. He spent a second or two checking numbers and making adjustments, then he started to climb back up the rocks.

Now Frud understood and followed him. Worm went too. They weren't leaving him here on his own, not in a place like this.

Soon they were back at the knobbly crown of dark rock that ringed the inner valley, scrambling about after Pig as he tried to find a good vantage point. Suddenly he flapped them down with one hand. Worm and Frud dropped on their stomachs obediently. It was like a gunfight at the OK Corral. Then he gave the thumbs-up signal.

He'd got what he wanted. The Bearded Wonder was standing on the track down, staring up at the rocks. He still didn't trust those little sneaks to have gone home.

Pig was all ready for him. He dropped a small stone. 'Ping' it went, as it bounced down the scree, the little sound magnified by the rocky walls all round. The man looked straight at him. But Pig was well hidden. All the man could have seen was the late afternoon sun flashing on a camera lens, all he could have heard was a tiny click as the shutter fell.

Seconds afterwards the boys were on the way down again, and Pig was big with triumph at his own cleverness.

'You're brilliant,' Worm said to him, as they picked their way down the mountain. He'd never thought he would say a thing like that to Pig Baxter, but you had to admire genius when you saw it.

Nobody said much as they made the steep descent. They had to concentrate. After all the rain in the morning the footpath was slimy with mud. But when they were back on the road they all talked at once, and this time Pig managed to keep up with them. Excitement had given him a second lease of life.

'Do you think they were the men the police were after?' Worm said.

Frud shrugged. 'I can't make my mind up. They were pretty nasty but we were in their tent. What do *you* think?'

'I don't know. There was that box, and they didn't look like outdoor types, did they? And they certainly changed their tune when we mentioned the police.'

'When *I* mentioned the police, you mean,' Pig said sharply. 'I'm going to get this film developed tomorrow, so the police can see it. They'll probably do it themselves.'

'But you've only taken one picture,' Worm pointed out. 'What a waste.'

'Not if it leads to something. Anyway, I've got three more rolls.'

'That was quick thinking,' Frud said generously. 'You got us out of a sticky situation there, Paul.'

Pig beamed. 'Well, someone had to say something. Anyway, what about that box?'

'It did look like the kind of thing you might have with you if you were after rare eggs. They've got special little compartments inside them—they have to be made by hand.'

'Pity we didn't get away with it before they came back.'

'We've got to remember everything,' Frud said. 'There was that map in the tent, with all the arrows on, and all that food. They'll be going over new ground each day, till they find the peregrines. Still, if the authorities know where the nests are they'll set a watch on them, I should think. They may not know yet though.'

'There were three of everything,' Pig said suddenly. 'Wonder where the third one was?'

'There were only two beds though,' Worm chipped in. 'And only two sleeping-bags.'

'Yes, but I saw three plates, and three knives and forks, *and* three mugs. They were in a tin bowl, by the stream. Don't say you didn't notice?'

'I didn't,' Worm said, feeling small.

'No good going in for this kind of thing, Worm, if you miss little details like that,' Pig said, sounding like a headmaster. 'That's the kind of thing the police want to know.'

Quite the little detective now, aren't we? Worm was thinking glumly. Come back, Sherlock Holmes, all is forgiven. He was fed up at the way things were going, annoyed that Pig had somehow taken complete command of the situation and was obviously going to report everything to Derek Giles. He'd like to have done that, but so far he'd not done anything positive at all. He had been too unnerved by that man grabbing him.

As they walked into the trees below the hostel Frud stopped for a last look at the mountains, before branches blotted them out. 'We might be lucky tomorrow,' he said. 'The weather's settling. See how high those clouds are now. Look, Worm, that's the footpath we took, up to those rocks.'

Worm trained the binoculars upwards. He found the jagged wall of rock that marked the tiny upper valley where they had found the tent, then moved the glasses along the path. From here it looked like nothing bigger than a string of raindrops under a gate. Then he saw something else.

'Look, who do you reckon that is?' Somebody was moving along the fellside, quickly and smoothly, as if on wheels. A small red blob growing bigger. 'Do you think it's Brian Blake?'

Frud snatched the glasses from him and looked. 'It's certainly very like him. I told you he didn't go up the Easemere Pikes today. Wonder where *he's* been?'

13

Worm felt miserable. The minute they got back Pig went off to tell the warden about the men in the tent, and Frud went too. They didn't wait for him. Frud was so anxious to get all the details right that he'd chased after Pig, in case he mixed anything up.

And Worm was jealous. Frud was his friend. Pig had come with them because he was older, but now it was turning into Pig and Frud, with Worm on his own.

He removed his sodden shoes and peeled his socks off, wringing the muddy water out of them; then he went to sit on the grass, by the beck, and stared glumly into the water. He was still there much later when Brian Blake walked up.

'You look wet. There's a drying-room you know, next to the kitchen. You can hang all your things in there, overnight,' he added helpfully.

'Thanks,' said Worm. 'Where've you been today? Anywhere interesting?'

'Oh, you know, round and about,' the man said vaguely.

'Did you get up the Pikes then?'

'Er, no. Cloud was a bit low, first thing, so I stuck below the tops. See you at supper. Must rush. Fish and chips tonight. Get those at home, do you?'

'Now and again,' muttered Worm.

He found Dot and Millicent in the drying-room; they sat side by side on two old chairs with their feet stuck in bowls of warm water.

'Hello, Peter, you look glum,' Dot said. 'You look as if you've lost a pound and found 2p. Where are your friends?'

'Oh, talking to the warden. When did you get back?'

'About an hour ago. We've got blisters. Gert told us to soak our feet, and she's given us some stuff to put on them.'

'She can't be all that bad then.'

'Oh, she just wants us fit, for tomorrow,' Dot replied, swishing her feet around and inspecting her orange hair in a small mirror. 'She *says* we're going up the Great Easemere Pike.'

'What's that?'

'It's one of the biggest mountains in the Lake District.'

'It'll kill me,' Millicent announced solemnly. 'If I get to the top I'll have to stay there.'

'We can always roll you down,' Dot said heartlessly, combing her hair.

'Oh you are *awful*.'

'How's the trombone?' Worm said, sitting on the floor.

'All right. How are the chest-expanders?' Millicent replied quietly. Worm blushed. He had noticed her peering in at him when he'd been having a quick five minutes after breakfast, before everyone had set off for the day.

'All right.'

'*Chest-expanders?*' Dot repeated.

'Peter's a fitness freak. I saw him doing his exercises this morning.'

'Are you in training for something then?'

'Oh, no, well, not really. Only, our school's taking part in a big race this summer, it's for the whole town. I want to qualify for it.'

'I wish I was as thin as you,' Millicent said mournfully. 'I bet you're a good runner.'

Worm couldn't think what to say. He was so used to people poking fun at him he'd expected these girls to make a big joke out of his early-morning exercises. They seemed to think everything was funny.

'Why have your friends gone off and left you then, the rotten things?' Dot inquired, in a motherly voice.

Worm hesitated. They hadn't agreed *not* to tell anyone else about the men in the tent. Anyway, these two might have their own ideas.

'Go on, you're dying to tell us,' Millicent said, drying her toes carefully. 'Go on, spill the beans.'

So Worm told them everything.

Dot fiddled with her hair as he talked, but Millicent never moved a muscle. Her small bright eyes were riveted to his face, and he could see her clocking the facts up, one by one, as if she was a kind of human calculator.

When he'd finished she frowned, and looked at Dot.

'What do you think?'

'Dunno.' She started sawing at her nails with a file.

Worm could see that *she* didn't think it was very exciting.

'Those three *plates*,' Millicent was mumbling to herself. 'And why on earth camp up *there*? They must have someone else in league with them, to pass the goods on to.'

'In *league*... *goods*... Honestly, Mill, you make it sound like something on the telly,' Dot said with a titter. 'They're only pinching a few birds' eggs.'

Worm looked at her with distaste. That's what Pig had said, at first. They'd be good companions for each other. He half-wished he'd kept the story to himself now.

But Millicent was interested. She was putting her shoes on thoughtfully, and muttering to herself. Then she stood up suddenly and gave Worm a very straight look.

'You know what I think, don't you?'

'What?'

'I think we should keep an eye on Action Man. It occurs to me that he may not be all he seems.'

'Who's "Action Man"?'

'*Brian Blake*, of course,' Dot and Mill said, in chorus.

14

The file on Brian Blake was started after supper. Worm, Pig and Frud met the two girls in the Quiet Lounge. This was a small, sparsely furnished room where you could go to read, or play cards. Pig printed ENGAGED on a piece of paper, and stuck it on the door.

'Surely you can't do that?' Worm said. 'It must be against the regulations.'

Official Rules frightened him, there were so many at Darnley Comprehensive.

'Oh, it's all right. I told Derek we wanted to map our route out, for tomorrow.'

(It was 'Derek', now, not 'the warden'. Pig Baxter was just like his father.)

'You might have waited for me.'

'Sorry,' Frud said, sounding embarrassed. But Pig just ignored him.

'We told him what we'd seen, and showed him where the tent was, on the map. He's giving my film to the postman tomorrow, and he'll drop it off in Windermere. He was pleased about that,' he added smugly.

'What's he going to do?'

'Well, he's already rung the police, and they're off first thing tomorrow, to check it all out. They do seem to think we might be on to something. Only, they'll have to find the eggs, or they can't prove anything.'

'We asked if we could go with them,' Frud added, 'but he said no. He thought the fewer the better, and I suppose we'd only slow them down.'

'But he did think the local newspaper would probably get to hear about it. That'd be something,' Pig said.

'What about Brian Blake then?' Millicent broke in suddenly.

'What about him?'

'Well, Dot and I think he may be helping them.'

'So do I,' said Worm.

'Him?' Frud said. 'Oh, I don't think so.'

'How can you be so sure? We thought there was something odd about that man the minute we saw him. All that stuff about a wife and two sons in Oldham! Do you really believe it? And have you noticed how much he eats?'

'I don't see what that's got to do with anything,' Frud said, though it had occurred to him that Brian Blake's excuse for not doing the Easemere Pikes was a bit weak.

'People eat too much for all sorts of reasons,' Millicent went on seriously. 'It says so in all the diet books. He eats very quickly, about three times as much as anyone else. It's guilt, that is.'

'And his clothes are so old,' Dot added. 'He told Gert he was a factory manager, but his sweater's got great holes in it, and he obviously can't afford to run a car. Didn't you tell us he came here with you, on the bus?'

'I think it's quite possible he's a man on his own,' Millicent resumed. 'There's money to be had in selling these rare eggs to collectors, we all know that. What's to stop him coming up here every April and doing the same kind of thing? Perhaps he takes rare chicks too, and sells them. He obviously knows this area like the back of his hand. And he *looks* so respectable, that's the point. He might have a whole lot of people waiting for eggs and young birds, it could be a really big organization, international and everything,' she finished breathlessly.

Worm thought hard about Brian Blake. There were definitely things about him that didn't add up. He was friendly enough but he never talked to you for very long. He was always saying, 'Well, must dash,' or 'Well, I'd better go and tidy up.'

Tidy up *what*? And dash *where*?

And he *had* lied to them about climbing the Easemere Pikes. He hadn't gone up those mountains at all. He'd walked up the same valley as they had. And they'd seen him through the binoculars, racing down.

But he looked so healthy, so normal, a man who loved the mountains and enjoyed nothing better than long solitary walks over the fells. The idea of Brian Blake as a criminal in league with those two men just didn't seem possible.

But Millicent had already produced a notebook and written on the cover: THE FACTS ABOUT BRIAN BLAKE.

These went as follows:

1. Origins doubtful. Does he really have wife and family in Oldham, Lancs.?
2. Compulsive eater. Possible guilt feelings.
3. Lied about plans on Day One. Was seen returning (late) from site of suspicious tent. Plate and cutlery possibly his.
4. Reads from thick book covered in *brown paper*.
5. General evidence of three people in tent. Eggs possibly passed to 'B.B.' for sale and disposal.

CONCLUSION: 'B.B.' possible *third man*.

Millicent read it all aloud, then shut the notebook. 'I'll keep this. Let me know if there is anything to add. Meanwhile, we must all keep our eyes open.'

Frud obviously didn't believe a word of it. He had a habit of switching off when things really irritated him, and he'd just switched off Millicent. He was looking through one of his nature books and writing notes of his own.

But Pig was excited. This was turning into a real detective story, like one of the late-night films his mum let him watch on television, when his father was travelling abroad. Worm knew all about that.

There was a large map pinned up on the Quiet Lounge wall, and a black arrow right in the middle of it, pointing at Great Easemere Pike. PLEASE NOTE AND BE WARNED said a handwritten notice THERE IS NO WAY UP THIS MOUNTAIN THROUGH JACKSON'S GULLY.

Worm had heard that name before. It sounded

like a place in a western, somewhere full of skeletons where men had starved to death during the Gold Rush.

'Somebody fell off that, last year,' Frud said quietly, looking up from his book. 'Two boys went climbing without the proper gear, and tried to take a short cut.'

'What happened?' asked Worm.

'He died. He broke his neck.'

Nobody said anything for a few minutes, but it was impossible to squash Dot.

'Gert's taking us up that mountain tomorrow.'

'Oh, it's quite safe,' Frud said, 'so long as you watch the weather and don't do anything stupid, like going off the paths. I climbed it last year with my dad and our Graham.'

'I thought we might go up there too,' Pig said. 'But on second thoughts perhaps we won't. I don't think I—'

'Come with us,' suggested Millicent. 'I'm sure Gert wouldn't mind a few more tagging along, especially somebody who's done it before.'

'What would she say, do you think?' Worm asked.

'Oh, "Jolly good," I expect,' said Dot.

Eventually some older boys came and turfed them out of the Quiet Lounge. They were doing a big walk the next day and wanted to spread maps out on the floor. Worm was just going through the door, last as usual, when a gang of six-footers hurled themselves through it, collapsing into the armchairs and all laughing loudly. He was glad to get out alive.

Pig and Frud had disappeared, together presumably. They were probably talking to Derek Giles again. Perhaps Pig had dreamed up some all-important piece of evidence about those two men. He'd really got his teeth into this egg-stealing thing now. You'd think there was a million-pound reward on offer, the way he was behaving.

The youth hostel was very quiet. Worm hung about miserably in the brown shiny corridor, wondering what to do with himself. Then Dot appeared round a corner, followed by Millicent. They both had coats on.

'Been abandoned again, Peter?' Dot clucked, like an old hen. 'Don't know why you bother with those two, especially the older one. He's awful.'

'I know. Frud's all right,' he added loyally, 'but he's bird crazy, so he's taking all this very seriously.'

'So are we,' Millicent said, peering over Dot's shoulder. 'That's why we're going out.'

'Going out? Now? At this time? But it's getting late. You might get locked out.'

'No, we won't.' Millicent looked at her watch. 'It's early. Anyway, we've got nearly two hours before lights out. Gert's given us a free evening. Why don't you come with us?'

'Oh, no, I don't think so,' Worm muttered, shuffling his feet. 'I mean what if—'

'Oh, *rubbish*,' Dot told him, 'you're coming. Get a kagoule or something, and we'll wait outside for you.'

'But where are we going?'

'On a little trip.'

The little trip took them down to the main gate and along the road, right away from the mountains. It was quite dark, but the sky was clear and the moon was shining. Worm looked up at its big silver face and something stirred deep inside him, something good. Moonlight, he was actually walking by moonlight, no street-lamps, no shop-signs, just the moon. He liked it.

'Where are we—'

'Shh,' Millicent whispered sharply. 'Look, there he is, straight ahead. Come on, we'll have to keep in to the side of the road, if he turns round he'll see us.'

It was Brian Blake. They could see his gaunt outline, his black hat, black stick, black breeches, all silhouetted in the moonlight. He was walking quite slowly for him, no doubt enjoying the fine starry night, like Worm. No need to rush.

Then they saw him look down at his wrist, and an object under his arm started slipping down. He tucked it in firmly, grasped his stick, and began to stride out.

Worm, Dot and Millicent crept out of the shadows and stared down the road.

'Come on,' Dot said. 'We mustn't lose sight of him,' and they moved forward.

'He's carrying something,' Millicent whispered, 'something quite big. It's under his left—no—his *right* arm. Remember that.'

'What for?' Worm asked.

'For the file, twerp.'

Dot was ahead of the other two. She made remarkably fast progress tacking across the silvery narrow road, in view of her blisters and her high-heeled shoes. She just hated walking boots, she said they made people with thin legs look like Mickey Mouse. 'Buck up, you two, or we'll lose him,' she kept saying. But they didn't. Journey's end was almost in sight, and as they tiptoed round a bend they were just in time to see Brian Blake stroll up to the open door of a little stone pub called the White Hart.

All three stopped dead in the middle of the road. Millicent was disgusted. 'The pub? Is that all? We've followed him all this way and he was just going for a pint? Well, of all the—'

'Don't faff, Mill,' Dot said coolly. 'We don't know why he's here, do we? We can find out, and while we're here we may as well have a drink ourselves. I've got some money. What do you fancy, Peter?'

Worm was taken aback. 'I don't drink,' he stammered. 'I mean, I don't want anything.' He sat down on a bench outside the pub, feeling distinctly confused.

'It's all right, I didn't mean a double whisky,' Dot said, getting her purse out. 'But I'm sure they'll sell us some lemonade or something. If we don't buy anything they might think *we're* suspicious. D'you want some crisps, Mill? Salt and vinegar flavour, or crispy chicken?'

Worm peered through the pub window as Dot stalked boldly in through the front door of the White Hart. Then he felt Millicent pulling on his arm. 'Let's go round to the side,' she said. 'We're too conspicuous out here at the front.'

He followed her round towards the back of the pub. Their shoes crunched so loudly on the gravel he was sure someone inside would look up and see them. But there was a lot of noise inside. A darts match was in progress and some people were singing round a piano. Brian Blake wasn't there anyway—perhaps he'd done a bunk already.

100

Then, 'Look!' Millicent hissed in his ear. 'Over there, in that doorway. It's them!' Worm peered through the little side window. Through a door marked SNUG he could see an emptier inner room, with trestle tables and high-backed seats like church pews. Sitting in one of them, swilling down a glass of beer, was Brian Blake, and he was talking to two men. One of them was large and most definitely bearded, the other was half hidden by an old wooden pillar that propped up the ceiling. But Worm could see green nylon and a bobble hat. It had every suggestion of mountain gear.

'Are those the men?' Mill said. 'The ones you saw?'

'I... I think so,' Worm stuttered. 'It looks very like them, but they keep moving about, and it's so smoky in there. I can't quite see their faces yet.' He pressed his nose to the glass and looked harder.

This atmosphere of intense concentration was shattered by Dot who came up munching crisps noisily and carrying a tray. In the excitement she slopped lemonade down Worm's neck. He spun round, stood up, and collided with her.

'Cool it, Pete,' she said cheerily. She was in a good mood now. It was quite jolly inside that pub. 'Seen anything then? Got any good clues?' She didn't sound all that interested to Worm. Her 'little trip' had just been an excuse, he reckoned, for a visit to the White Hart. She wanted a bit of night-life. She probably knew where Brian Blake was going, all along.

Yet there was Millicent at his feet, tense as a rubber band, squatting down in the damp gravel, trying to collect vital scraps of evidence for her notebook. She was in earnest, and Dot was just taking her for a ride. Worm resented that. He got down beside her again for another look. He'd stick up for her.

And this time they saw something. 'Look,' Mill squeaked. 'Just look at that. He's giving them a parcel, it's that thing he had under his arm. It's a kind of large package, it's wrapped in polythene.'

'Open it... Open it...' Dot urged loudly through the window. She was interested now. But the man with the beard didn't. He just grinned at Brian Blake, made some funny remark, then put the package inside a rucksack.

'What's happening now, for heaven's sake?' Dot said. 'The window's steaming up, I can't see properly.'

'I can,' Mill answered, in a tight voice. 'They've given him some money, I'm sure they have, and— and he's getting up, he's leaving.'

'He might just be going for another round of drinks,' Dot said. 'You can't jump to conclusions, Mill. This is serious.'

Nobody said anything for a minute, then Millicent put her arm on Worm's sleeve. 'What do you think, Peter? You saw them up the valley.'

'I don't know, I can't decide. If only that pillar wasn't in the way. Tell you one thing though, see that hand, holding the beer glass, in the green kagoule? Well, it's definitely... pudgy? Don't you think? I'd put that in the file.'

'Everything's got to go in,' Millicent said seriously, as they began to walk back, and that was *all* she said. She needed her breath for the two-mile trek up to the hostel. They hadn't left too much time for getting back, and Worm was terrified of being locked out.

He didn't want to get into trouble, and he didn't want to tell the other two about his visit to the pub. They'd gone off without him again, so they could do without his piece of information. It might just turn into a race, to see who nailed Brian Blake first.

If he did keep quiet, and work it all out on his own, he'd only be following Frud's advice, he'd only be sticking up for himself. 'Worm against the world'—it sounded quite good, that did.

15

Worm wasn't used to all this fresh air and the next morning he overslept again. He woke up in the middle of a dream in which a monster was bellowing, 'Jolly, jolly *good*!' as it chased him down a mountainside.

When he opened his eyes the noise was still going on: Millicent, practising 'Frolic'.

Straight after washing-up the three boys went to see the warden again, though Worm held back at first, and Frud knew why. He'd been very quiet at breakfast, and a bit sulky. 'Come on, Pete,' Frud had said. 'Sorry I disappeared last night, but you've got to watch Pig, and what he says. I had to make sure he told Derek Giles the truth, and no more.'

So Worm did go, but he didn't mention his walk to the pub. That was his secret, for the time being.

They were disappointed when the warden told them he'd got up at first light, walked up to the hidden valley, and found no tent.

'But we did see them,' Pig insisted. 'We went inside and everything, and we saw that case for the eggs.'

'I'm sure you did,' Derek Giles said calmly, looking

at the boys with his keen, brown eyes. But Frud thought he didn't believe them.

'There was a fire,' he said. 'We saw a big black ring on the grass.'

'Oh yes, I saw that. But anyone could have made a fire down by the tarn—other people will have camped there.'

'They said they were spending three days there,' Worm said. 'And they've gone.'

'Yes,' the warden said slowly, but that was all.

'Listen, if you think we're just having you on—' Pig spluttered indignantly.

'Now look, boys, I wouldn't have got up at the crack of dawn and gone all the way up there if I thought that, now would I? I'm just saying there was no tent. All right, I agree, that's suspicious in itself, if they told you they were there for a few days. I know you're disappointed, but in a case like this you have to play your cards carefully. It's quite possible you put the wind up them, and they scarpered. There. Had you thought of that?'

'Well, no,' admitted Pig.

'The police will have your photo by tonight. It was a shrewd move that was, it may prove a great help. So just keep your eyes open and report back to me if you see anything else.'

'So there's nothing more we can do?'

'Not at the moment. Enjoy these mountains, that's what you've come for after all.'

'We just wondered if anyone else had brought you any information,' Frud said slowly. 'Has, er, Mr Blake seen anything, for example?'

'No, not so far as I know. Don't see a lot of him, of

course, he's not around much. He always wants to make the most of his day.'

'Yes,' Frud replied thoughtfully.

Ah ha, Worm thought, so Frud's getting suspicious too. Well, he just might tell him about last night, when they were walking, as long as he didn't tell Pig.

As they turned away the boys noticed someone looking at them. A window was open in the warden's little office and you could look through into the field, next to the hostel. Derek Giles had his back turned and saw nothing. But Pig did. He watched the skinny, tanned frame of Brian Blake slide past silently and slowly, the way you do when you don't want anyone to see you, but when every word matters.

And Millicent had seen him too, through the dormitory window, sweeping the fell-tops with his binoculars and writing things down in a notebook. It was a fine, clear day and the weather was settled. There was no real need to keep checking and double-checking, surely? Any fool could follow a clearly marked path today. What was he looking for? Perhaps he was signalling to somebody up there; he might even be using the glasses. You could flash morse-code signals with lenses.

'Eavesdropping in early morning, outside warden's office', Millicent added to the facts about Action Man. 'D. Giles reports: "Keeps himself to himself." Excessive use of binoculars. Fair weather. Suspicious. Signalling in morse?' Then she added a detailed description of what she'd seen in the pub. The file on Brian Blake was getting thicker.

'Good-o!' said Gert, when Pig, Frud and Worm asked if they could join St Hilda's on their climb up Great Easemere Pike. 'We'd be glad to have you. Much jollier doing something like this in a group, don't you think? Glad to see that you're showing our two wilting lilies how to walk.'

The wilting lilies were Millicent and Dot, who had trailed at the back yesterday when Miss Pringle took them over Easemere Crags. They were in a lower form than the others, and they stuck together, though Millicent walked so slowly even Dot grew tired of sitting on boulders, waiting for her to catch up.

Gert had got it firmly into her head that Frud's name was Hank.

'No, Miss Pringle, his name's *Frank*, Frank Hudd,' Dot kept saying.

'Hank? And I'm told you've been up this mountain before, Hank? Jolly good. Perhaps you'll walk at the front then, with me.'

'She's a bit deaf,' Millicent explained to Worm. 'That's why she shouts. It's a waste of time telling her to call him Frank.'

'Frud won't bother.'

'Pig doesn't like his name, does he?'

'Why do you say that?'

'Well you tend to call him that under your breath, I've noticed.'

'It's not a very nice name, is it?' Dot remarked.

'Neither is Worm,' said Worm.

The clouds were high, the sky a clean blue, and there was a breeze. 'Enjoy this, you lot,' Frud shouted to them, as he ran ahead to join Gert. 'It's a day in a million.'

Worm watched him move into the lead. There wasn't going to be much chance to talk to him about Brian Blake. He didn't like being left right at the back with Pig and the two girls, but Miss Pringle had ordered him to keep the party together from the rear. She seemed to think he was one of hers now, and she was dead bossy.

'And remember, *no stragglers*!' she warned, looking pointedly at Millicent and Dot. She clearly thought they were pathetic.

'We'll get up there,' Mill said, in a determined voice, 'even if it takes all day.'

Probably will, Worm thought, the speed you walk.

Local people called the Easemere Pikes the Two Sisters. An ancient legend told of two young girls who fell in love with the same shepherd boy. When he died, in a wild snowstorm out on the hills, the sisters wept together. The gods took pity on them and changed them into mountains, so they could stand there for ever, looking helplessly down into Easemere Vale for their lost love, weeping into the little streams that tumbled down the fellsides and into the great lake itself.

The warden had told them the story last night. Pig thought it was soppy but Worm didn't. It filled him with a kind of poetry. He wasn't going to tell Pig though.

Frud and Miss Pringle led the way round the lake and skirted the foot of Easemere Crags. Then the track widened out. It took them through a broad valley with gentle hills on either side. The two mountains were at the end, rising up gracefully in purple and blue, out of the light spring green of a small meadow. It was such a clear day the track to the top looked like a broad chalk zig-zag.

'Can't you hurry up a bit?' Worm said anxiously to Millicent. 'We don't want to lose our way. We might get separated from the others.'

Dot cackled loudly. 'Come off it, Pete, we're not so stupid. That footpath looks like the M1.'

Worm tried to speed them up even so. While they were on the flat part they had enough breath to talk as they went along. Without Dot, Millicent was even more serious. She told Worm how she hated being fat, and how some of the girls at school called her 'Barrel'. 'They sing "Roll Out the Barrel" sometimes, when we're getting changed for PE,' she confided, as they puffed along. 'I do hate it. Mum puts me on all these salad diets but I get so hungry. You are lucky, not having a weight problem,' she added, looking enviously at Worm's thin legs.

'No, but there are other things.'

'What d'you mean?'

And quite suddenly Worm found himself telling Millicent the story of his life, how they'd always called him Worm, and about Dad getting killed on the motorway, and about the fish and chip shop. He told her how happy he'd been at the Junior School with Frud, but how much harder it all was now, at Darnley Comprehensive.

'You see I'm not much good at school work. I can't remember things, and the teachers always say I get hold of the wrong end of the stick. I make stupid mistakes. That's how I came to ring the fire-alarm.'

He gave Millicent a quick sideways look. This was a trap. There was a spiteful side to Pig Baxter and Worm was certain that he'd have told Dot and Millicent all about Wrigley's famous fire-drill. But he hadn't. This was clearly the first Millicent had heard about it. She listened carefully to the story of that dreadful morning, then she said, 'But, Peter, that's what I'd have done. What if there *had* been a fire?'

'But there wasn't, and everybody laughed.'

'Ah, but there might have been. Look at it that way. You made a fool of yourself for the sake of something important.'

That was exactly what he'd wanted to do, something important. And it was what he still wanted. Only next time there would be no mistake.

The broad footpath was gradually narrowing and getting steeper. Ahead of them Pig and Dot slowed down as they wound their way up the real mountain. Their voices floated back on the wind. Pig was so engrossed in what he was talking about he seemed to have forgotten his aches and pains. 'Fantastic,' he was saying. 'And do you remember that bit when the coffin was unscrewed and it was all *green*? Oh, I've seen that three times—no, four. I've got my personal television in my bedroom, 24-inch, digital.'

Millicent was listening. 'They seem to be talking about all the films they've seen in the last ten years,' she said. 'Dot lives at the cinema, more or less.'

Worm looked at Pig's hunched-up shoulders and watched his fat hands waving about as he talked. Then he saw him take some money from his pocket and count it. (Who but Pig Baxter would take a wad of fivers up a mountain?)

'That's no problem,' Millicent heard. 'My father gave me loads.'

'Those two are plotting something,' Worm said.

16

Frud reached the summit of Great Easemere Pike in record time, and a few minutes later Gert galumphed up after him. They sat peacefully together and looked at the views, while, one by one, the girls from St Hilda's reached the pile of stones on top, and collapsed all round them. It was a good half hour before Worm, Pig, Dot and Millicent showed up. Everyone stood and cheered them on loudly as they laboured up the last few hideous feet.

'Don't even *speak* to me,' Millicent said in a faint voice, sagging down next to Miss Pringle. After exchanging a few knowing looks with Pig, Dot arranged herself on a flat rock and calmly began to eat her sandwiches.

Worm walked away from the others and found Frud standing on his own, inspecting a great rocky outcrop with his binoculars.

'Sorry you had to stay at the back,' he grunted. 'But it wasn't my idea. I bet those three slowed you up terribly. Here, do you want to borrow these? The views are fantastic.'

'In a minute,' Worm said. He just wanted to look.

From down in the valley the mountaintop had looked mossy-smooth. Close to it was a minefield of murderous boulders. The land fell away sharply on nearly every side. On his right he looked down the spine of a mountain range, all knobbled and bumpy, like the back of some gigantic dinosaur. On his left the land was gentler, range upon range of green, humpy fells, flattening out towards a blue-black glimmer that was the sea. Through the binoculars he could see a spit of land—the Irish coast, so Frud said. Only now was he aware of the great height. As they'd walked up Easemere Vale, then wound on to the summit ridge, with the sun beating down on them, he'd not been nervous about the climb. He had not given Blackstone Edge a thought, and that was a pimple, compared with this.

The wind blew against him, snatching up the girls' chatter and flinging it over the fellside like a handful of dust. He stood and stared in complete silence, thinking of their small, stuffy house behind the shop, in Darnley. All the years he'd lived this had been waiting for him.

He felt very alone. It was so marvellous he wanted Mum and Patsy to share it too. Most of all he wanted his dad.

Suddenly Worm's eyes filled with tears. He removed Frud's binoculars carefully and handed them back. Then he walked over to the others, rubbing at his cheeks and giving a big sniff, to calm himself.

But Frud pulled at his arm. Silently he pointed to the huge mass of rock that stuck out from the side of the mountain, down below.

'Did you see that?'

'Yes. It's Jackson's Gully, isn't it? I can see it looks easy to climb.'

'It *looks* easy, but it's a death-trap. I've just seen something fly out of it.'

'Not a peregrine falcon?'

'I think so. Well, it could be. Keep your voice down, though.'

'Good job those men aren't around to hear you,' Worm whispered.

But Pig Baxter was around, and he'd heard everything.

He was not at supper. Neither was Dot Marsden. Nobody noticed till the warden waved his soup ladle and said, 'There's a lot left over. Isn't anyone hungry tonight?' It was then that Worm saw the three gaps— Pig, Dot and Brian Blake.

'Millicent,' Gert boomed, 'go up to the dormitory, please, and see what's happened to Dorothy.'

'Where's *your* friend?' Derek Giles asked Frud. 'Doesn't he want any supper either?'

'I'll go and get him,' Worm said, sliding off the bench. He was suspicious.

'Where's Mr Blake?' Miss Pringle asked the warden.

'Oh, he didn't order supper tonight,' Worm heard. 'He said he'd get something in a pub, on his way back.'

In the dormitories Worm and Millicent found exactly the same thing: clothes rolled into a bundle and stuffed down the bed, under the blankets, to make the shape of a sleeping person, and a hurriedly

114

written note that said: 'Gone to Windermere, to cinema. Will hitch back.'

'What are we going to say?' Worm asked Millicent, as they met at the top of the stairs with the notes in their hands.

'The stupid things,' she answered. 'Honestly, I feel like telling Gert. This is *just* like Dot.'

'I told you they were up to something,' Worm said. 'Pig's been rabbiting on about being bored, and going to the pictures, ever since we arrived.'

'Well, we'd better make some excuse for them, I suppose,' Millicent replied fiercely. 'But I think it's really *mean* of them.'

Back in the dining-room Gert was eating another bowl of soup. Without Pig and Brian Blake there were seconds of everything, even thirds. Millicent announced in a matter-of-fact voice, 'Dorothy's lying down, Miss Pringle, she's got a sick headache. I think it was the sun.'

'Right-o. Thank you, Millicent. I'll leave her for an hour or so; perhaps she'll feel hungry later.'

'Oh, she was almost asleep, Miss Pringle. She has some special pills for these headaches, you know. I should think she'll sleep till tomorrow now.'

Worm was full of secret admiration for this smooth quick-thinking. It made him falter even more as he muttered something to Derek Giles about Pig feeling sick. He could feel himself going red.

'Hope it wasn't our packed lunch?' the warden said cheerily, trying to unstick sausages from a tin.

'Oh, *no*,' Worm managed to get out. 'Only, he ate rather a lot of sweets today.' It was pretty feeble, but it was all he could think of.

He passed Frud the note, under the table.

'Makes you sick, doesn't it? How on earth are they going to get back?'

Frud was really annoyed. Pig Baxter was supposed to be looking after *them*, not the other way round, and if he got into trouble the warden might tell them *all* off. He could even confiscate their youth-hostelling cards, and make a fuss to their parents. It was just like Pig to do this. Selfish.

Worm was thinking exactly the same thing.

'Hope they get locked out,' he said to himself, looking down at his bangers and mash.

17

They did.

It was 'lights out' at half past ten, and after that you were supposed to be quiet, so everybody could get some sleep. No one had checked up on Pig. Some of the groups had moved on, so that apart from the three boys the only person using the men's dormitory that night was Brian Blake, and he hadn't come back either.

Millicent managed to stop Gert in her tracks, as she bore down on the hump in Dot's bed. 'She had to take another pill, Miss Pringle, her head was so bad. I don't think she'll want any supper. She said she'd be as right as rain by tomorrow. Really, I'd leave her.'

Then one of the older girls came up to report that she'd lost her purse, and Gert was sidetracked into organizing a hunt for it, otherwise Millicent thought she might have given 'Dot' a hearty shake. She had that look in her eyes.

Worm was still awake at midnight. He sat up in bed and looked out of the window, across the flat, neat blankets of Brian Blake. The brown-covered book Dot had seen him reading was lying on the floor, under a pair of gym-shoes. Worm picked it up and slid it under his own pillow. It was too dark to see what it was, but he would have a good look in the morning.

He stared out into the night. The fellside behind the hostel was silvered with moonlight and he could hear the beck splashing over the stones. After the din of Darnley the silence was unnerving. But Worm liked it.

Sounds travelled great distances when everything was so still. They were two miles from the road, but he could clearly hear a car engine, then doors banging. Half an hour later he saw and heard what he'd been expecting, a circle of torchlight bobbing along the path, then being flashed up at the dormitory window; gravel crunching under someone's feet, then hitting the glass. Somebody was giggling too. They were back.

Worm opened the window cautiously and peered out. Dot and Pig stood below, next to a line of dustbins. Pig was wearing his flashy orange kagoule, and Dot had her high-heeled boots on.

'We can't get in, Peter, everything's locked up,' she whispered. 'Can you come down and unbolt the back door?'

He hesitated. To get there he would have to creep past the warden's flat, and Derek Giles had a large dog. It would be just his luck to knock something over and set the animal barking. Then the whole hostel would know what was happening.

It was cold out of bed. He felt like shutting the window and leaving them outside for the night. Then he thought about it. Frud, who was snoring gently, would never do a thing like that, however much he disliked someone.

Neither could Worm. He stared down at them thoughtfully. The ground didn't look so far away. The hostel was a chalet-type building with a low roof. They could climb up, with a bit of effort.

'Look,' he whispered back. 'If I let you in downstairs we'll wake the dog up. Why don't you try climbing up here? You could use the dustbins.'

'Aw, come on, Worm,' Pig whined peevishly, 'I'm cold. I'm not climbing up there. Surely you're not scared of a dog?'

'I'm *not* scared of it. It'll bark, that's all. It barks at everything. Are you ready, Dot? I'll give you a hand up.'

Dot had already managed to lift one of the empty bins into a space below the window, and had quietly put a lid on. Now she was standing on it, handing her shoes up to Worm.

'Give me a hand, will you, Peter,' she instructed coolly. 'And brace your feet against something when I pull.'

Worm couldn't see much outside, but he felt Dot pulling on his arms, tugging at them sickeningly so that she almost screwed them off. He heard her thud against the side of the hostel, grunting with the effort of getting herself off the bin lid. Then her face popped up in the window-space, and she hurled herself forward, collapsing on to Brian Blake's empty bed.

Pig was shorter than Dot, and much less agile. Between them she and Worm tried to grab hold of his arms and haul him through the window, but he was nervous about losing his balance. He just stood there dithering on the dustbin lid, waving his arms towards the roof, but not reaching nearly high enough.

'Come on, Paul you'll really have to *stretch*,' Dot whispered firmly. 'Get a move on, we'll pull you in.'

But in the dark Pig lost his bearings. He thrust his arms up all right, but instinctively put a foot out, at the same time, and fell sideways heavily. There was an almighty clang. His foot had gone into an empty dustbin and it toppled over slowly, rolling towards the others that stood in a line outside the kitchen door.

The bins clashed together like gigantic cymbals. A dog started yapping wildly, and lights came on downstairs. Pig crawled out of his dustbin smelling of old cabbage, picking a dried-up tea-bag out of his hair.

Frud sat bold upright in bed, and felt round for his glasses, but then the door opened and the light went on. Someone of great bulk charged across the dormitory in a vast Viyella nightie, and peered into the gloom.

'Need any help, Mr Giles?' a familiar voice bellowed. 'I think we've got truancy on our hands!'

'Oh, no,' Dot whispered to Worm as the great voice split the darkness. 'It's *Gert*!'

But they were all packed off to bed remarkably quickly, when Derek Giles marched up the main staircase with Pig shambling behind him, scarlet-faced and complaining loudly that he smelt of dustbins.

'Whose fault's that?' the warden asked curtly. 'Get into bed. You can wash the smell off in the morning, and you can wash all your bedding too.' When all the lights were off again he held a conference with Gert, out on the landing. Worm listened hard, but could make no sense of the low mumbling. Even Miss Pringle was talking in whispers.

Next morning two storms broke.

Millicent and Dot were imprisoned in the Quiet Lounge with Gert, and this time she didn't bother to keep her voice down. Creeping past to the drying-room, to do a few exercises, Worm heard words like 'deceitful' and 'stupidity' and 'a disgrace to the school'.

'I'm very sorry, Miss Pringle,' Millicent was saying, 'I just didn't realize…' But Dot actually seemed to be arguing, and the louder Gert spoke the louder she argued. 'We weren't doing any harm,' Worm heard. 'It was only a bit of fun.'

'*A bit of fun!*' Gert was bawling. 'You might have been out there all night. Heaven knows where you might have ended up, hitching lifts from lorries. You're the most irresponsible girl I've ever taught and, what's more, you had no right to involve your friend.'

Well, that was something. At least Millicent wasn't going to get too much blame for shielding Dot. And when Derek Giles summoned the boys into his office after breakfast he said much the same to them.

Pig wouldn't look at the warden. He stood between Frud and Worm, glowering at his feet. It had taken him a good hour to wash the bedding and peg it out to dry. After that he'd been given a brush

121

and sent off with Dot to sweep the rubbish from round the dustbins. Only then had they been given some breakfast, when it was lukewarm and congealed on its plate.

'I'm surprised you did such a stupid thing,' Derek Giles said. 'Anything could have happened to you. There are very few vehicles going along these mountain roads at night, and the way over the pass is high. If the weather had changed you could have been in real trouble. Besides, I trusted you to keep the rules. I don't expect people to come here and make use of what we offer, then go sneaking off at night. We don't want people like that staying here.'

Pig's cheeks glowed. Worm actually felt sorry for him. They all liked Derek Giles, and Pig had been more eager than anyone to track down the egg-stealers, taking the film out of his camera and telling him all about the men in the tent. Now everything was spoiled.

Enlarged photographs of his snapshot were already pinned up all over the hostel. Underneath each was written: HAVE YOU SEEN THIS MAN? THE POLICE WOULD LIKE TO QUESTION HIM ABOUT ACTIVITIES IN THIS AREA RELATING TO WILDLIFE. And there was a long list of phone numbers.

The warden saw Pig looking at them.

'Yes,' he said gravely. 'And you were the boy who was so helpful about that. I'm really disappointed in you, Paul.'

'Any more developments, sir?' Worm whispered, feeling he was back at school with all its rules and punishments.

'Not so far, nobody's had a sighting of them yet.

I've got some leads as to where the birds might be though; we thought they'd moved on, this year.' As he said this he exchanged a quick look with Frud.

Pig noticed. He opened his mouth, then shut it. Derek Giles felt rather sorry he'd been so hard on him, he looked quite crushed.

'What will you do if you find the nests?' he asked, after a pause.

'Oh, a watch will be set on them, they'll be guarded. But, of course, that takes time to set up. We're off the beaten track here, you know.'

'I see,' Pig said thoughtfully.

Worm was watching him; he knew Pig Baxter better than Derek Giles did and he could see that his brain was doing overtime. He was perking up too. His mouth had that firm, set look that said he was working an idea out. Pig was up to something. Worm didn't know what though.

Much earlier they had got the best piece of incriminating evidence so far, about Brian Blake, and Millicent had collected it. It was a good job she saw it happen, and not Pig. Nobody would have taken him seriously, after the dustbin saga.

Gert had made all the girls write home. She'd produced fourteen identical postcards of Easemere Lake and sold them all a first-class stamp. 'Put it in the hostel box tonight,' she had ordered them. 'It's by the shop. The milk wagon collects the post very early, and takes it down to the village. Got a pen, Stephanie? Millicent? Good-o.'

Millicent wrote: 'Dear Mum and Dad, Hostel not at all bad and weather quite good, for round

Don't faint but I climbed a mountain today. Tomorrow we're supposed to be "relaxing"(?). Boating, if fine. Have practised every day, sixth position improving. Love, Millicent.'

But in all the fuss about Dot and Pig going off like that she'd forgotten to take it down to the box. Something woke her just after six—water running in the men's cloakroom, just along the corridor from their dormitory, then a door banging. She sat up in bed, wide-awake, with the other girls snoring all round and Gert a pink Viyella mountain in the bed under the window. Then she spotted her unposted card, lying on her trombone case.

She got up, took it, and crept downstairs, and as she went past the door of the common-room a noise stopped her; it sounded like a lot of papers falling on to a polished floor. She peeped in through the glass panel in the upper half of the door.

Brian Blake was standing in front of the notice-board with his back to her. As he bent down to pick the papers up she heard, 'Oh *damn*,' and she noticed he was fully dressed, with his walking jacket on, his breeches, and his thick woolly socks, everything but his boots.

He was carefully pinning the notices back on the cork board, each one perfectly level, four drawing pins to each sheet. He was pernickety over small details. That was suspicious in itself—master spies were supposed to be fussy in the same way.

But what on earth was he doing? It was only quarter past six.

Millicent pressed her nose to the glass and saw him remove something from the notice-board. He took it over to the window, examined it carefully, then slipped it inside a notebook he'd taken from his pocket.

He was making for the door now. Millicent retreated and backed up the stairs. Half-way up she poked her head out and stared along the main corridor. Now she could see him moving towards the bench by the warden's office, and sitting down to lace his boots up. Then he was off, sliding the big brass bolts back very slowly, shutting the heavy door behind him, stepping out into the crisp morning.

Millicent came back down the stairs and went into the common-room. The cork bulletin-board was a masterpiece of tidiness. Ten out of ten for its neatly positioned drawing-pins and its notices with all their edges parallel. WHAT TO SEE IN LAKELAND stood side by side with RULES FOR WALKERS and RULES OF THIS YOUTH HOSTEL. Slap in the middle was the warden's recent appeal for information about the egg-stealers. HAVE YOU SEEN THIS MAN? Millicent read, and saw a red paper arrow pointing down dramatically to a price-list: 'Two tins of mushroom soup for the price of one—special offer at the hostel shop.'

But Pig's photograph of the Bearded Wonder had gone.

18

It was their last day at Easemere. Tomorrow St Hilda's were moving on to another hostel, and the boys were going home. Worm had to go to Blackpool first, to meet up with his mum and Patsy.

'What are we going to do?' Pig said in a subdued voice, joining the other two by the stream.

'Well, I've decided to go into Windermere with the girls,' Frud replied. 'Miss Pringle invited me. They're planning a boat-trip on the lake, and there's a big wildlife exhibition I'd like to see. It's my last chance.'

'Am I invited?' Pig said doubtfully. 'I'd like to go shopping.'

'No,' Frud said. 'And I don't think there's room in the van anyway.' He sounded quite annoyed. He didn't want Pig following him round the exhibition, he'd say it was boring. They'd end up doing the rounds of the coffee shops in Windermere, if he came. Frud could just see it.

'Come on, girls,' Gert was shouting. 'Into the minibus everybody. Dorothy, where are you? At the front, please, where I can keep an eye on you. Coming, Hank? And what about your little friend?

126

Would he like to join us? We could just about squeeze him in.'

That's me, Worm thought, I'm just Frud's little friend, I'm an afterthought I am.

'No, thank you,' he called across to Gert, 'I think I'll stay round here today.' It wasn't that he was sulking but he really didn't want to go traipsing round Windermere with St Hilda's School and the woman Gert. He wanted to spend his last day in the valley.

'Come *on*, you two,' Gert boomed, as Dot and Millicent scuttled across the car-park. 'Whatever it is can wait till we get back.' As they rushed past Worm the file on Brian Blake was thrust into his hand.

'Read it,' Millicent whispered. 'Recent developments.'

As the white van bumped off into the trees, Worm opened the notebook. To THE FACTS ABOUT BRIAN BLAKE had been added:

7. Did not spend Night Two in hostel. Was observed in Willow Café, Windermere, by Pig and Dot, talking to two men in suspicious circum-stances. Close resemblance to men in tent detected (see also White Hart episode, above).
8. Not at breakfast on Day Three.
MASTERFACT:
9. Removed photo of bearded suspect from hostel board (witness: M. Wilkinson). Left early, 6.15 a.m.

Note: Regret—Evidence of Peter Wrigley discounted. Book in brown wrapping found to be *The Southern Fells* by A. Wainwright.

'Here, you have this,' Worm said to Pig, shoving the notebook into his hand. He felt stupid because of the brown-paper-wrapped guide, and bewildered by all the other details. 'It just doesn't add up to me. I did think that book might give us a clue to what he's up to, but it's only a tourist's guide.'

'Well, he'd still need one out here,' Pig said, 'even if he was helping those men, and it was him we saw in the café, after the film.'

'He's just not the type,' Worm insisted. 'That's what Frud thinks, and I agree with him; I just can't believe that bit about taking the photo. Millicent must have got it wrong.'

'You can never trust anyone,' Pig said sharply. 'People aren't always what they seem. My dad's always saying that.'

'Well, why don't we tell the warden he's taken the snapshot then? And if you really did see the three of them in Windermere we should report that too, and we should show him the file.'

'*No*,' Pig said, 'absolutely not. These are still only suspicions, Worm. Think of your case. It's got to be watertight, and we mustn't say another word till we're quite certain. Not till the picture's complete. And if you go blabbing *I'll wring your neck. See?*'

'All right, all right, give over, will you?' Worm shook his arm off and wandered away. He knew what Pig was after now. He wanted the glory. The moment would come when he'd go sneaking off to Derek Giles, with all his facts neatly assembled on a plate. Nobody else would get a look in then, Piggy boy would have it all sewn up. He had the style to go with success, the camera, the boots, the cash, the posh accent.

Who'd listen to Worm if he came up with anything?

He felt black. Frud had deserted him and it was their last day in the Lake District. He didn't want to leave this quiet valley and go back to Darnley. The thought of the town suffocated him.

He wandered up to the hostel and collected his packed lunch from the kitchen, then walked down the path to the lake. Ten minutes later Pig rolled up complete with rucksack, kagoule, and swimming gear.

'Derek says you can swim at the far end. Coming?'

It was 'Derek' again now. Pig and Dot Marsden were two of a kind, nothing crushed them for very long.

'Don't think so,' Worm said. He wasn't much of a swimmer. 'Anyway, what have you brought all that clobber for, if you're just going swimming?'

A sly, shut-in look crept across Pig's face. 'Oh, er, thought I might do a bit of a walk later on. Might see what Action Man's up to.'

'Have you seen him then?'

'No, but he's gone up towards the Pikes. I looked in the "Walks Book" in the common-room, where you're supposed to leave a note of your day's route. You can come with me if you want,' he added ungraciously. He obviously didn't want Worm tagging along.

'No thanks.' Who wanted to go on a walk with Pig Baxter?

The weather was dry again, but the air was close and speckled with midges. It felt more like midsummer than April. Pig plunged into the water and squealed at the cold, then he struck out towards a tiny island covered with long grass and a few stunted trees. He swam like a fish. Worm watched enviously, thinking of the fabulous swimming-pool in Dickie Baxter's moorland garden. Some people were lucky.

He'd brought a book with him, and the chest-expanders. When Pig went off for his walk he might do a few exercises quietly, by the lake, then have a read. There was nobody about.

His leg muscles had hardened up and he was feeling much fitter than the day they'd left Darnley. The walking didn't make him breathless any more so it had been worth coming, even if he never got into the Race.

For the moment he just wanted to sit by the lake, taking in the colours and shapes of the mountains so that he would remember it all, when he was back in Darnley. Soon the sunshine and the quiet lapping of the water made him feel drowsy. He'd only had about five hours' sleep the night before, and he lay back on the grass. A few minutes later he was snoring quietly.

A cold gust woke him up. He looked at his watch and discovered it was half past twelve. The remains of a packed lunch were scattered close by. Worm looked at them in disgust, that was just like Pig. He never lifted a finger at home, his mother did every little thing for him. Then he noticed that the torn sandwich-bag had writing on it, and was held down by a stone. It said: GONE UP THE PIKES.

Worm glanced up the valley. He could just make out a small orange blob moving along the mountain path, then vanishing somewhere near the bottom of Easemere Crags.

A cold feeling came over him as Pig disappeared. He was certain that he was off to investigate those rocks by Jackson's Gully, where Frud had seen the peregrine falcon. Pig had asked him all about it yesterday, on the way down the mountain.

He wasn't sure why he was going though. He surely wouldn't want to steal rare birds' eggs for himself. Worm couldn't believe that he would want to go egg-stealing at all.

It must be a case of *hurt pride*. If he could locate the new nests, and report back, the warden and the police might think better of him. Perhaps if he brought them some vital information they wouldn't tell his father about the trip into Windermere, and getting locked out. Derek Giles had hinted he might do that.

Brian Blake might also come into it. Perhaps Pig hoped to catch him with those men, camped out somewhere the warden hadn't investigated.

But he was daft to have gone off like that. The hostel was full of notices advising you not to go climbing alone. If you had to they warned you to tell somebody exactly where you were going. Pig wasn't like Action Man. He was a rotten walker, and he didn't know the first thing about mountains. It was a stupid thing to do.

Then Worm did something equally stupid. He should have gone back to the hostel and told Derek Giles. Instead he got up, collected his things together, and went after Pig.

19

He walked rapidly the way Pig had gone, trying to remember the hints Frud had given him. Go at a steady pace, watch where you're putting your feet, never cut corners, take your time.

But as he rounded Easemere Crags he felt time was against him. The weather was slowly changing, and for the worse. A cold wind blew down from the fells, giving him goose pimples, and he noticed some cows lying down in a field.

The sky was darkening too, turning from tin colour to a dirty yellow. The two peaks at the end of Easemere Vale had become gaunt, dark shapes rearing up against mottled clouds. His eyes swept the path for a fellow walker, but the valley was empty. Worm might have been the only person alive on earth.

Except for Pig. An hour later, when Worm reached the foot of the mountains and began the real climb, he looked all round anxiously for a sign of the orange kagoule. But the fellsides were bare. He put his hands to his mouth and shouted, 'Hello! Pig! Hello! Where are you?'

He listened hard for a reply, but there was silence; then, as he raised his hands to call again, he heard a faint mutter of thunder, far away.

Trying not to listen to what the weather was doing, Worm toiled up the path. For a couple of hundred feet it zig-zagged across a beck that bubbled down the mountainside over great white boulders. Then it petered out, and he was faced with a scramble up a rough rock-face. At the top of this the footpath started again.

He had not really noticed this rocky wall the day before. It had been different then, with the sun out and sheep staring down at them from precarious ledges. All his energies had been absorbed in getting Millicent and Dot up to the summit, and he had covered the ground without thinking.

Now most of the sheep seemed to have bolted for cover and, as he clawed his way up the rocks, a cold rain spattered his face. His feet were hurting through the school shoes, and he felt tired already. He could kill Pig Baxter for leading him a dance like this.

On the path again Worm paused to get his breath back, and looked up at the two Easemere Pikes. The wind was blowing strongly now, and the sky was greenish. As he stared at the twin peaks, and at the massive craggy outcrop of Jackson's Gully, he saw the cloud drop suddenly, thickening to mist, sweeping down over the mountain with the speed and force of a great flood.

His heart turned over. This was what all the books warned you against. This was what must *not* happen, to be out on a mountain alone, in bad weather, with no compass, no food, no protection. And no clue left down below, to show where you had gone. They were both fools.

For a few minutes Worm stood perfectly still and tried to get his bearings. If he went on climbing he would eventually reach Heaven's Gate, a narrow plateau of scrubby grass between the two summits. It took its name from the miraculous views you might have, if you were up on the fells on a clear day. Yesterday they had all stood there on the way down, and Gert had lectured them about the five separate valleys they could see from the windy ridge.

She had also pointed out the first-aid 'station'. You couldn't miss it, a white coffin-shaped chest with a red cross painted on it, set in a bed of concrete just under the lip of the plateau.

'Why is that there?' Pig had asked.

'It's for silly people who try to climb up Jackson's Gully,' Frud had explained solemnly. 'There aren't many of them. You always have to cater for the idiots though.'

Worm went on, leaning his whole body against the mountain as the wind ripped at him. On Heaven's Gate he didn't dare stand up. A gale was blowing across the gap between the peaks with such force it could have plucked him off the ground and hurled him down the fell.

Someone had daubed a flat rock ahead of him with white paint. One crude arrow pointed to Great Easemere Pike, another to Little Easemere Pike, and underneath Jackson's Gully was a big cross and the words NO ENTRY! The cloud hung over everything and Worm could only see about ten yards round him. The dirty mist swirled over him and he listened again for Pig. All he heard was thunder, getting nearer.

He sat down in the shadow of a gigantic boulder, all huddled up, cringing away from the battering rain, looking up towards Jackson's Gully, trying to decide what to do. And suddenly the mist parted down the middle like a pair of curtains. He could see the mass of rock, a rough-hewn cluster of black stumps, rearing up at him like battered organ pipes. In the tingling light it looked as if the whole mountain was falling forward to crush him.

Worm stood up and clung to the rock. He opened his mouth to shout 'Pig!' but his voice was drowned by a huge thunderclap, a noise so violent he felt the earth shake beneath him.

Then something flew past him, so close he could hear the beat of its wings. The falcon was calling, a strange, high-pitched squealing noise, more like a mouse than a bird of prey. Lightning split in two over the rock, and the huge thunder came again, almost instantly.

As the deafening noise died away Worm heard a scream, and down the dark, jagged line that cleft the gully he saw Pig falling, a bright orange blob that dropped off a ledge, bouncing as it moved downwards, thrusting out arms and legs in a kind of sickening slow-motion.

The fall dislodged small stones that trickled down gently after him, making the sound of waves retreating on a pebbly beach. He lay sprawled out, only feet away from Worm, still moving slightly, a bright heap in the rough grass at the bottom of Jackson's Gully, with the wind plucking at him, threatening to blow him off.

There was another, fainter, thunderclap, and the rain thickened to a downpour. As Worm inched along Heaven's Gate towards him Pig raised one of his arms slowly, then began to scream again.

20

As Worm reached him he grew quieter, then let out a strangled sob. 'I was trying to get down, when the thunder started,' he began. He spoke as if it was the most natural thing in the world for friend Worm to appear out of thin air, half-way up Great Easemere Pike, in the middle of a storm. He was used to people dancing attention on him. 'I found a nest, and I was climbing down. Then one of them flew out at me and I—*oh*, it's my *leg*, my *leg*…' He began to scream again, louder than before. His round face was all wrinkled with pain. Worm sat down on the grass and tried to put an arm round his shoulder, but the small movement made Pig cringe.

'*Don't*, don't *touch* me, I can't *bear* it.'

He had screwed up his eyes into nothing, and the tears were spurting down his cheeks. Worm stretched his hand out helplessly and put it on top of Pig's. They were both as cold as ice.

'I must go and get help,' he whispered, when the noisy crying had lessened slightly, and the pain seemed to have eased.

'What about me?'

'I'll just have to leave you here. What else can I do? I can't carry you down. It looks to me as if your leg's broken. Did you hit your head when you fell?'

'I don't know, I don't know,' Pig moaned.

The picture of Pig bouncing down Jackson's Gully ran through Worm's mind again, speeded up, in vivid technicolor. It would be a miracle if he hadn't banged something very badly, but he couldn't see any blood in his hair. His arms and legs were darkening to a bluish-pink. In an hour or so Pig would be a mass of bruises.

He knew he should leave the boy where he was, because of the broken bone and because he may well have hit his head when he fell. Pig was just too shocked to know what had happened to him in the last ten minutes. He was lying at the end of the grass plateau, under a chin of rock that jutted out from underneath the great crags. At least he was out of the wind a little.

Then Worm remembered something. 'I'm going to that first-aid station, that box with the cross on. There'll probably be some blankets in it.'

'Don't leave me, Worm,' Pig cried hopelessly, trying feebly to move the damaged leg. 'If I could only… Oh… No… *Please, Worm*…'

And after that there was no problem about leaving him alone for a minute. His head had lolled sideways, in a dead faint.

Worm crawled along the ridge on all fours, because of the tearing wind. There was a small door in the side of the box. He opened it and crept inside. He could see all kinds of cartons piled up at the far end, and there was a horrible musty smell over everything.

He didn't bother with the boxes but grabbed a polythene sack that looked as if it contained blankets, and humped it over his shoulder. As he shut the door he noticed a canvas stretcher. He debated for a second, but left it where it was. He wouldn't be able to lift Pig on to it on his own, and moving him might be dangerous anyway.

Through the lashing rain he crawled back to Pig, terrified in case the wind took the weight of the sack and pushed him off the mountain with it. It took him a long time to cover the hundred yards of grass; he had to inch his way ahead bit by bit, only moving when there was the slightest lull in the storm.

Pig was moaning now, and thrashing his head about. When he heard Worm's voice he half opened his eyes. 'Why doesn't someone *come*?' he kept saying drunkenly, as if his mouth was full of broken teeth.

'I'm going for someone, but I want to make you comfortable first.'

Somehow, Worm managed to get Pig out of his sodden kagoule and swaddled him in blankets, rolling him over very gently to get them underneath, so he wasn't lying on the wet ground. The slightest movement made him cry out, but Worm had to take the risk. The greatest danger was that he would get too cold. When he had finished the boy looked like a fat cocoon, with a ridiculously small head poking out of the top.

He took off the bobble hat Mum had knitted him for the holiday, and pulled it down over Pig's reddish curls. Then he spread the big polythene bag out over him, on top of the blankets, and weighted it down with rocks.

As he walked away to find the right track down he looked back for a minute. 'I'm going down into the valley for help,' he shouted. But this time Pig did not reply.

The wind had blown the tops clear and Worm had the two dark summits at his back, glowering at him as he picked his way down. Soon he had plunged into mist and could see only a few feet ahead. It was as if he was above the clouds, in an aeroplane.

He kept thinking of Pig lying unconscious on the mountain, and about all those notices in the hostel: IN CASE OF INJURY SEND FOR HELP. DO NOT LEAVE THE INJURED PARTY. STAY TOGETHER IF POSSIBLE.

If he'd stayed with Pig someone might have come down from one of the Pikes eventually; but they might not. Anyone who had listened to the weather forecast would have been wise to remain in the valleys that day, and nobody knew where the two boys had gone.

It was no use agonizing, now, about whether he'd done the right thing. He must go down. If he came back and found Pig dead he would know his decision had been the wrong one. It was horribly simple.

Please, he said to himself, as he descended, please let there be someone down below, to help us. Last time he'd prayed like that somebody had played a trick on him. Don't let it be like that now, he thought, almost in tears with anxiety.

When he was on the flat again, below the rock wall, he looked back. There was no wind at this level. The two Pikes were still free from cloud but below them was a thick yellowish band of mist. It looked as

140

if someone had dragged a huge paintbrush right across the fellside, and somewhere in the middle of it Pig was waiting for him.

It took him another half hour to reach the valley head. After the rapid descent his legs ached horribly, and he was cut and bruised all over.

In Easemere Vale it was clear of mist, but raining heavily out of a sky the colour of pea-soup. Nobody in their right mind would be out in this. All over the Lake District they'd be huddled by walls and in bus-shelters. At Easemere they'd be waiting for Derek Giles to come and open up, so they could join the queue for a hot bath.

Then, half-way down the valley, Worm thought he saw something. He began to run. After the stony mountain tracks the broad footpath felt like a city pavement. He had never moved so fast in all his life. As he caught up with the walker his heart was pounding hard enough to split his chest open, and there was vomit in his mouth.

First what he had seen was a mere splash of red. As he ran and hollered it became a flapping square, then a person with a rucksack on his back, plodding along the valley towards the youth hostel.

'Stop! Stop! For heaven's sake *stop*! Someone's injured up there, we need *help*!' As the walker turned round Worm skidded in the mud and collapsed on the path, clutching at the red jacket to stop the man in his tracks.

'Hold on, son, what on earth's the matter?' said a voice Worm knew. He was looking up into the brown, puzzled face of Brian Blake.

After the agonizing run he was suddenly sick on

the grass. Action Man took hold of his shoulders firmly and held him up, otherwise he looked as though he'd fall flat in the mud again. Then the man took out a big handkerchief and mopped Worm's face.

'Now then,' he began kindly, 'you'll have to sit down for a minute, you look done in. Why don't you just get your breath back. I—'

'There's no *time*!' Worm screamed at him. 'Don't you understand? Pig's up there, on Heaven's Gate, in the storm. He fell off Jackson's Gully. I think he's broken his leg.'

His thin voice rang out down the lonely valley, half a shout, half a sob, but harsh, and very desperate.

'Who's Pig?' the man said calmly, as he pushed Worm towards a huddle of big flat stones by the path and made him sit down.

'That boy who's with us, the fat one. He's been looking after Frud and me, on this holiday.'

'And who's up there with him?'

'Nobody.'

'*Nobody?* You mean you left him up there, *on his own?*'

'I had to. There was no one to stay with him. He went off this morning, he was looking for birds' nests. But I never dreamed he'd go up the mountain, not all the way up there.'

In spite of his panic, Worm's wits hadn't quite deserted him. He looked hard at Action Man when he said 'birds' nests', but not a muscle reacted in the lined, brown face. He just stood over Worm, in the middle of the path, looking first along the valley bottom through the rain to where the track disappeared in a smudge of trees, then back at the mountains where mist was wreathing itself like white rags round the dark peaks.

'Go back,' he said suddenly. 'You must go back.'

His voice was different now; it was expressionless and hard. He threw his pack on to the ground and took a pair of old plimsolls from a side pouch. He shook his boots off and pulled the runners on instead, then he removed his jacket and a thick sweater. In the end he stood on the path in plimsolls, tatty red sweatshirt, and khaki shorts.

But even now he was methodical, unhurried. Worm watched him pile his gear up and hide it behind the boulders.

'It'll be all right there. The farm next to the hostel has got a Land Rover. If there's anyone around I'll get them to bring me back here in it. The track's wide enough. It'll save some time.'

But Worm wasn't listening. His eyes were riveted to what Brian Blake had put on top of his folded jacket. It was a box. The man had been carrying it under his arm when he'd skidded up to him on the path. It was inside a clear polythene bag and he could see the brass catches and the little lock. It was an egg-collecting box.

'What's that?' he whispered numbly, pointing to it.

Brian Blake hardly glanced at it. 'Oh, that. Just something I picked up, earlier today. Look, it isn't important. Are you ready?'

He was limbering up on the path, as if he was in a race, waiting to take his mark. 'You must go straight back up there, son. It'll be going dark before too long. If you're there before me, don't move him, and don't budge from that spot. I'm going to ring the mountain-rescue team, and alert people. Then I'll come back. I'll probably catch you up. But just start walking.'

For a minute Worm forgot Pig. Why was he being sent back? Why didn't Action Man go himself, and leave him to make the phone call? He was suspicious.

'But why can't I ring them?'

'Look, they've got to be told at once. I might just run a shade faster than you, I've had a lot of practice. But I *will* come back. Meanwhile, you must get to your friend, just in case there's any snag at this end. I know it's a lot to ask, you must be tired. But you *must* do it. How long were you coming down?'

Worm looked at his watch. 'An hour and a half, just over.'

Brian Blake whistled. 'From Heaven's Gate? That's pretty good going I'd say, well, it's fantastic. You must be a tough one.'

He gripped Worm's shoulders hard. 'Go on, go back. You can do it. I'll be up with you just as soon as I've made the phone call.'

Worm watched him tearing down the valley, amazed at his speed. Pig had sneered and said Brian Blake was old enough to be his grandfather but Worm didn't think he'd ever seen anyone run so fast, except on the telly. He'd get into any big race, unless the police caught up with him first, and clapped him into gaol.

In a kind of weightless dream, unable to say whether he was sleeping or waking, Worm turned and went back up the mountain for the third time in twenty-four hours.

21

He didn't know how he was going to get back to Pig, he was so weary. The rain had turned into a slow monotonous drizzle and although he was walking quite fast Worm was trembling with cold. Everything he had on was sopping wet. His thin hair was plastered to his head and freezing water was trickling down his back, inside his jumper, making his spine crease with shivers. But at least he was moving, at least he was alive. Better to be on the go than to be like Pig, lying perfectly still on a bare mountainside, while the wind raged round him. He might die of exposure.

Worm screwed up his eyes and pushed the terrifying thought to one side. He wouldn't think about that. It must stay on a shelf in his mind with all the other painful things he couldn't bear to remember: Steve Weir's bully boys, the fire episode, Dad's crash. He must simply keep on walking, one step at a time.

At least his legs weren't aching, not yet anyway. Frud had been right about that, the more you walked the easier it got. But he did have an awful stitch, like a knife-blade being pulled down through his breastbone, splitting it neatly.

There was still a fair distance to cover on the flat before the real climb started and he felt exhausted already. He wanted to sit down on the path, to curl up in some wet grass and go to sleep. Anything, rather than climb up there again.

Perhaps it was like pain. 'Think of something else,' Mum always advised him, when he had to have a tooth drilled or an injection. 'Think of something nice, like eating your favourite dinner in front of the telly on a Saturday night. It won't seem so bad then.'

Worm tried singing. That's what Frud did to take his mind off things, he hummed little tunes. It might make the time pass quicker, make him forget how sick and exhausted he felt. But Worm didn't know many songs. He tried a few jingles from the TV adverts, 'Elasticated nappies, They really make you happy,' he piped feebly. 'They're fun to eat.' No, *no*, that was the crisp one. 'They do not *leak*, They're quite…' but he couldn't remember the words. So he tried one for breakfast cereal, 'Ya godda gedup in the morning, uh uh, When ya see the sun is shining, uh uh…' But his reedy treble soon fizzled out, like a damp firework. It was hopeless. Singing those daft tunes didn't lull him into any kind of calmness, they couldn't take away the rasping pain in his chest, or the hardness of the stones through his thin soles, or the icy hand that kept thrusting itself down his back making him shudder with cold. He would just look at his feet from now on, that might help.

'Left, right, left, right, and before you know where you are you're nearly there. Come on, Peter.' Who'd said that? Dad, on a summer holiday in North Wales. Worm was five, their Patsy only a baby, and he and his father had climbed a hill behind the seaside resort. It wasn't a mountain, just a little green knoll above the town, but to Worm it was Everest. And Dad had said, 'That's the way, one step at a time, my goodness you're going to be a grand little walker.' He was so gentle. If his father was walking beside him now they'd be on Heaven's Gate in no time.

But nobody was there to walk by his side. Worm was alone. Frud was in Windermere with Gert and St Hilda's, Pig was up on that mountain, probably unconscious. Dad was dead.

He wanted to cry but he stopped on the path and gave himself a good shake, rubbed the tears from his eyes, and tried to speed up a bit. No good turning the tap on, that's what his mother would say. And he was making a little progress now, another ten minutes' hard slog and he'd be on to the first rock scramble.

He turned and looked back. If Brian Blake had got that Land Rover to come out they might be on their way up by now. But the valley was empty. Well, of course it was, Worm told himself, trying not to panic, not even Action Man could have reached the hostel as quickly as that.

Would he come back though? Worm was racked by doubt. There was absolutely no mistake about the egg-container, he'd seen it himself on the pile of clothes, by those stones. Seconds earlier it had been tucked under Brian Blake's arm. And he'd not wanted Worm to make the phone call. 'Go back, *go back*,' rang in his ears as he crept painfully up the scree-littered fellside. Perhaps Millicent had been right, with all her wild suspicions.

The wind had changed yet again. As he laboured up the stony path he could clearly see the two Easemere Pikes and the green dip of Heaven's Gate between them. The gale had driven the creeping mist off the fell and Worm's way up was clear. But there was still a mile to go before he reached Pig. And it was the worst mile.

The track was getting rocky now, and very steep. The heavy rain had made the going treacherous, and both hand- and footholds were slippery. Worm clawed his way up blindly, almost on all fours in the tearing wind which buffeted him more and more savagely as he climbed higher. His hands were bleeding, his nails were broken and sore; the pain deep in his chest was surging up through his body, pummelling at his stomach, making him gobble at the air for breath; and when he opened his mouth to breathe it tasted as though it was filled with blood.

But he kept on going, a tiny yellow dot that inched its way upwards like a crawling insect, making for a minute patch of grass that splashed the brown-black of the fell with sudden green, and in the middle of it a jag of orange that was Pig Baxter. Thunder still rolled round in the sky overhead, the long mountain range sprawled out eastwards like a sleeping giant, and across its shattered face, an insignificant speck in that huge wilderness, Worm battled on, clinging, creeping, in the end almost hurling himself up bodily on to the narrow ridge, but not actually stopping till he had reached the little mound of blankets, had put out a hand, and touched it.

When he looked at Pig closely he felt horribly frightened. He was lying just as Worm had left him, all trussed up in the red stretcher blankets in the shadow of Jackson's Gully. But there was a dreadful stillness about him. His face was chalk-white and his eyes were closed.

'Pig,' Worm said quietly, then he started to shout, 'Pig, Pig, *Pig*!'

The boy's head lolled over horribly. He looked dead.

Worm loosened the covers and thrust his hand down the front of Pig's sweater. His chest felt warm and his heart was still beating. But Worm was terrified. He got hold of one cold hand and dug his nails deep into it. Then Pig shifted slightly, his lips parted and he let out a tiny moan.

Brian Blake had told Worm not to move him. He knew that anyway. But he couldn't just sit there staring at him. He had a weird feeling that Pig would die if he stared too hard. So he scrambled across to the first-aid station and got the stretcher. The mountain-rescue people would have their own special equipment but it may save time. If Pig was really badly injured there may be only a few minutes between life and death.

Worm didn't know how long he sat there, waiting for somebody to come—there was something wrong with his watch. It had stopped. The water must have got into it. But that time, with Pig unconscious at his side, was the longest and loneliest he had ever lived through.

He couldn't bear just staying in one spot, looking down at Pig and willing him to open his eyes, so he turned his back, swivelled round, and stared down the mountainside, watching the colour drain away from the fells, feeling the rain down his neck. Twice he saw a large bird fly out of a crack in Jackson's Gully and disappear into the valley. At least Pig had been right about something. He'd found the new nesting-place. That was all the good you could say about the hole they were in now.

Tucked into the shelter of the rocks, with the great crags glowering over him, Worm was more or less out of the wind. But it was dying out anyway, the whole landscape was softening and the mountains settling down into an evening of calmer weather.

He stood up and took a few steps forward, peering down to see if he could spot the rescue team. But the path immediately below was hidden by an overhang of grass and stones. He listened for voices, and for the crunch of boots on rattling scree, but nothing broke the immense silence all round him.

He stared out across the fells, sea-green, dark orange, black, patched with tattered shadows as the clouds moved overhead. The mountains looked almost alive, like great arms opened up to him. It was the wildest loneliness and beauty that Worm had ever known. As he looked he forgot about Pig, forgot his pain, his cold, his weariness. He gazed and his heart lifted inside him, and the endless shapes and swirls of the quiet land filled him with comfort.

22

Quite suddenly two things happened at once. A head popped up at the edge of the overhang, then a brown-green blodge appeared, separating itself slowly into two young men. One was tall and heavily bearded, the other thick-set and shorter, very strong-looking. Both had ropes wound round them and small rucksacks on their backs. The first head was Brian Blake's. He was still wearing his old sweatshirt and the ancient shorts. He'd only stopped in the valley to put his boots back on.

Worm began to shout and waved his arms furiously; all three spotted him, and waved back. Then they walked rapidly towards him. When he saw them close up Worm nearly fainted. It was *Them*, surely, Pudgy and the Bearded Wonder! He retreated, looking helplessly at Brian Blake, then back at the men. But the *police* were after this lot, they were *thieves*, they'd more or less threatened to bash the three boys up outside the tent. How could they...? Then he looked more closely. The smaller man was grasping his hand and grinning. 'Don't worry,' he was saying, 'here come the marines. You've done your bit.'

Worm's insides were caving in with relief. It was easy to see how he'd made the mistake. There *was* a resemblance to those men in the tent but these faces were different, older, full of humour, and very tanned. And they looked fantastically fit too, not a spare ounce of fat between them, like Brian Blake.

The bearded one had come up and was asking a lot of questions about Pig. Worm opened his mouth to explain but before he could get a word out a noise in the sky made them all look up, and eastwards. It was what they all hoped for, a low buzzing like an angry fly, a hum that got steadily louder.

A yellow blob had appeared in the sky above Little Easemere Pike. It was a helicopter. They all started to wave crazily and Brian Blake tore his sweatshirt off and waved that. One of the men took something from his pack that looked like a firework, and lit it. It was a flare, a distress signal flaming there on the dark mountain, showing the pilot where Pig was.

It took only minutes for the helicopter to reach Heaven's Gate but it was an eternity to Worm. As the machine hovered directly overhead the two young men unfolded the stretcher and lifted Pig on to it gently. Worm wanted to help too but Brian Blake held him back.

'It's all right, son, leave it to them. Get a bit of strength back, you've done more than your share.'

'You got back quite quickly then. Thought it might be dark before you came. How did you get these men to come so soon?'

Brian Blake looked at him, then at the men. Then he smiled shyly. '*These?* Oh no, this isn't the official

152

rescue team, they organized the helicopter. These two are my sons.'

'Your *sons*? But I thought… How…?'

'They're up in the Lakes to do some rock-climbing, staying about five miles from here. I'm a bit stiff for that caper these days, the wife and I just stick to the fells. No, I met up with them a couple of times in Windermere. I've seen quite a bit of them, on and off. Today they'd walked to the hostel. We were just having the one night together.' He grinned at Worm. 'Got myself locked out last night, I did. Came back even later than your friends. Warden ticked me off too. Quite right.' He laughed.

'I knew they were wrong about you,' Worm said, speaking his thoughts out loud.

'What d'you mean?'

Worm hesitated, then it all came out. 'We thought you might be one of those nest robbers. We were on the look-out for them. The warden asked us to keep our eyes skinned but it was all, y'know, hush-hush. Pig and Dot saw you in the café, and I saw you in the pub talking to, well, we thought it might be… the men the police were after. They were like your sons from a distance, sort of, and we never got a proper look.'

Brian Blake looked puzzled. 'But why suspect *me*?'

Worm took a deep breath. He may as well go the whole hog now. 'We noticed you creeping about,' he stammered. 'We saw how you went off early every day, all on your own. It seemed a bit suspicious to us. I'm sorry,' he added firmly.

It had to be said. Even now there were unanswered questions: the package he'd given them in the pub, the photograph, *that egg-box*. But Worm's bones told him Brian Blake was all right. He'd always known it really.

'Well, son,' Action Man said thoughtfully, 'you were right to suspect me in a way. You see, Derek Giles had told me to keep my eyes open too. I was doing a bit of detective work myself. We should have joined forces. That's why I borrowed your friend's photograph. Shouldn't have done it really. The egg-box was sheer accident; I found it today, coming down from their old camp-site. It's empty. I managed to get it open. They must have panicked and thrown it away. The police are hot on their trail now, apparently.'

Worm had gone whiter than ever. 'Are you all right?' Action Man was saying. 'Here, I've got a drink in this. Are you listening?' He wasn't, he was too busy thinking. The minute he got back he was going to find that file on Brian Blake, tear it up, and shove it in the dustbin. If Pig recovered he'd stick him in as well.

The pilot made three attempts on Heaven's Gate before he made a landing. The green plateau was only just wide enough, and it was difficult to keep Pig level on the stretcher, on the uneven ground.

'He's going to be all right,' the tall man yelled to Worm above the noise of the helicopter. 'I've seen quite a few cases like this. This isn't the worst by any means. He's not as bad as he looks. He tried to speak to us when we were getting him on to the stretcher, so don't worry. Best friends, are you?'

Worm didn't answer. If only they knew.

On his third swoop the pilot signalled that he was

going to come down. The noise was deafening and the helicopter blades sent a tearing wind across the fell, scattering stones and sucking at Worm's clothing.

Instinctively he clapped his hands over his ears. He hunched up to Brian Blake and watched as they manoeuvred the stretcher towards the opening in the belly of the machine. From inside hands reached down, grabbing for canvas straps. Instructions were yelled hoarsely, all but drowned by the roaring engine.

At last the stretcher disappeared inside. The man with the beard climbed up after it, turning to give Worm and the others the thumbs-up signal. Then the yellow slit closed and the helicopter rose up into the darkening sky. They watched it do a complete circle over the fells before going back on itself and making for the coast.

Brian Blake was shoving a plastic cup into Worm's hand, and a lump of cake. 'Here, get that inside you. It's ginger, the wife made it. I brought a great piece of it, but the boys took most of it for their packed lunches.'

Worm stared down at the sticky square. Ginger cake from the wife in Oldham, baked specially for the rock-climbers, and handed over in the pub. That put the tin lid on it. He daren't tell Millicent.

'Are you ready, Dad?' Tom said, the one that was left. He was looking anxiously at the shivering Worm, and so was Action Man.

'Listen,' he said kindly. 'If you feel you can't make it back we can carry you. There's another stretcher in that box.'

'No, I'll walk. I'm OK now.'

'Come on then, let's make a move,' Tom said. 'This boy needs a bath and a good hot meal.'

'And a medal,' Brian Blake added under his breath, '*and* a medal.'

Worm tried to get up but he couldn't. His legs had turned to jelly. Only now, when the helicopter was on its way to hospital, with Pig stowed safely inside, did he burst into tears, out of sheer relief. And Brian Blake put his arms round him and said it was all right now, just as Dad would have done.

23

Pig's mum and dad came tearing up the motorway in their new Mercedes. Vi Baxter collapsed when she saw her only son semi-conscious in the hospital, with his right leg encased in plaster from the hip to the toes and his face all blotched with hideous bruises. The doctor had to give her some tablets, to calm her down.

Worm spent the night with Frud, in the warden's flat, and in the morning he phoned his mother in Blackpool. Her voice sounded a bit wobbly because she'd heard a local radio bulletin about the accident which had made everything sound worse than it was. She was only convinced that Worm was in one piece when he told her so himself.

Mrs Baxter had rather more to worry about, but she needn't have. Pig came round properly late in the afternoon of his first day at the hospital, and was soon asking for something to eat. A few hours later he wanted his Walkman, and as soon as it arrived he ordered his mother to stop talking. He said it made his head ache, but really it was because he wanted to tune in to Radio One.

Dickie Baxter rang the youth hostel and arranged for the two boys to stay on till he could come and fetch them. St Hilda's were packing up. Worm nabbed Millicent. He wanted to have a quiet word with her, about Action Man.

The file on Brian Blake was at the bottom of her rucksack, so he couldn't throw it away, but he did tell her how wrong they'd been ever to suspect he was a thief.

Dot thought the whole thing was a laugh. She smiled knowingly when Worm explained about the two sons and their rock-climbing holiday, and when she heard about the ginger cake she laughed her head off.

'Oh, shut up, Dot,' Millicent said furiously. 'How were we to know it wasn't the same pair? They certainly looked alike from a distance, we all agreed on that. And I don't care what you say, that man did behave oddly. You said so yourself.'

Like a lot of clever people Millicent was not good at admitting she was wrong. 'I still think he was an extremely suspicious character,' she said emphatically, lugging her rucksack out into the car-park, where Gert was noisily loading up the minibus, 'creeping about like a private eye, listening in on private conversations.'

'How do you know he wasn't suspicious of us?' Worm said. 'He'd probably heard you talking about him. Perhaps he couldn't make head or tail of it. Had you thought of that?'

'What about all the eating then?'

'Oh, *Mill*,' Dot interrupted, 'why don't you let it drop? It was only a bit of fun, right from the beginning.

Some people eat a lot because they're greedy, like you,' she added unkindly.

It was clearly not a joke to Millicent, but she was defeated. She climbed into the waiting minibus without another word, pulling her trombone case in after her.

She was going to miss Worm. She wasn't at all surprised to hear that the small, insignificant-looking boy had saved someone's life. You couldn't always judge by appearances. You only had to talk to Peter Wrigley to know what he was like, he'd got guts and a lot of common sense.

As Gert started the engine Millicent rolled her window down and shouted, 'Good-bye, Peter, and good luck in your race. We might see you again one of these days. My dad sometimes comes to Darnley, with the band.'

She was very subdued all the way to the next hostel. As the minibus bumped down the track, and the waving boys disappeared for ever, Dot could have sworn she saw Mill actually brushing a couple of tears from her cheek. But whether it was because she'd just said good-bye to Peter Wrigley, or sheer frustration at being proved wrong about Brian Blake, she never would say.

Frud was really looking after Worm. Since his return from Great Easemere Pike, white, shaken, and looking like death warmed up, he'd hardly let him out of his sight. He kept disappearing into the hostellers' kitchen and coming out with cups of tea and baked beans on toast.

'I'll be getting like Pig,' Worm said, shovelling it all

down. 'I don't usually eat this much.' But he was pleased, all the same.

Secretly, Frud felt a bit guilty. He'd been rather selfish leaving Worm on his own, and going off to Windermere. He'd not exactly pressed him to accept Gert's invitation. And if they'd all stayed together the accident would never have happened. Frud knew how serious it had been. There were graves all over the Lake District, in little churchyards, marking the spot where climbers were buried, people who'd fallen off cliff ledges and been lost in blizzards and storms. Pig might easily have died up there. So might Worm.

'You'll come back, won't you, Pete?' he said anxiously, as they stood outside with all their gear, waiting for Dickie Baxter. 'We could come with our Graham next time. And why don't you join our rambling club? That'd keep you fit, they want good walkers, and you're obviously cut out for it.'

'I might,' Worm said cautiously, enjoying the sun on his face, the sparkle of the lake through the spring trees. Of course he'd come back. He could hardly bear to leave it as it was.

'They caught their egg-thieves anyway,' Frud said, almost as an afterthought.

'Why, what's happened then?'

'Someone saw that man on a train bound for Scotland. There *were* three of them. It was somebody who'd seen that photo of Pig's, stuck up in a post office. They phoned the police.'

'So they've got them?'

'Oh yes, and a lot of eggs, not the ones they were after here, but quite a few others. The police boarded the train at Carlisle and collared them, so the warden told me.'

'I hope nobody tells Pig that,' Worm grunted.

'Why not?'

'He'll be more big-headed than ever.'

Pig was going to have quite a long stay in hospital, so the Baxters decided to check into a big hotel in Windermere. When the doctors were quite certain that his son was going to be all right Dickie Baxter said he'd drive to Blackpool with Frud and Worm, collect Mum, Patsy, and Auntie Glad, and whip them all home in the Merc.

But before he left he insisted on taking Worm shopping.

'I want to buy you something, Peter,' he said. 'We can never say thank you to you properly for what you did for Paul, but I'd just like to give you a little present.'

As he was speaking his voice went all quavery, and he mopped his eyes with a big handkerchief.

Worm was horribly embarrassed.

'I don't want anything, Mr Baxter, honestly, it's all right.'

But he could have saved his breath. Dickie Baxter was used to getting what he wanted, he was like Pig.

An hour later they stood outside a mountain-eering shop.

'All right Peter, boots you want and boots you'll have. The best they've got. Just you choose a pair.'

Worm did. They were like Pig's, but the leather felt softer. He stroked it for a minute as the assistant looked round for a box.

'Somehow thought you might prefer to stay away

from those mountains for a bit,' Dickie Baxter said, writing out a cheque.

'Oh no, Frud and I are coming back. In the summer, if we can.'

Next stop was a huge gift-shop by the lake, where Worm was told to choose something for his mother. He knew it was no good protesting. He would have to explain that Dickie Baxter had insisted on paying for the present, and he just hoped she wouldn't mind. She didn't often buy things for herself.

He wandered round the shop, looking at the glittering displays of pottery and china, unable to make his mind up.

'How about a nice tea-set?' Pig's dad suggested. 'Or one of those ornaments? Take your time,' he said expansively. 'The money's no problem.'

At the end of the shop some paintings hung on a bare white wall. Worm went over and looked at them for a long time. Then he said, 'That's what I'll have. Mum would like that.'

The small painting was all gold and pink. At first it looked nothing more than a few swirls of colour dabbed here and there, but when you looked more closely you could see it was a picture of a waterfall, tumbling down into a clear, deep pool. The sun was shining on the water, in a dazzle of light, and in the spray two birds were flying close together. It was called 'Two Birds Circling in a Summer Dawn'.

Worm stared and stared at it. It was the kind of picture you felt you could walk right into. He could feel that water on his face, he could see that sunlight. He could hear those little birds calling to one another, for the sheer joy of living.

That was what he wanted to remember about the last three days. If he woke in the darkness again, as he had last night, to see old Pig near death on the mountain, and the huge crags falling down on him, he would think of that picture, and go back to sleep.

'Are you sure that's what you want, Peter?' Dickie Baxter was saying, in a puzzled voice. 'Your mum likes that kind of thing, does she?'

'She'll like this,' Worm said firmly, tucking the picture under his arm.

24

Those two presents were only the beginning because Dickie Baxter was a real Fixer. Although he was very busy in the next few months, driving all over the country in his car and making business trips abroad, he didn't forget Worm.

Unknown to anyone he was getting things organized. It meant writing to quite a few people, and having a long chat with his old friend Harold Spinks, a Darnley Town Councillor. He also drove across the Pennines to chat up a famous sports personality in his luxurious stone farm-house (with swimming-pool *and* view). Dickie quite fancied the place himself.

Worm, Frud, and eventually Pig all went back to school. It was a good term. Worm kept up with his exercises and got really fit. He joined Darnley Ramblers and went on long walks at weekends with Frud and his family.

And the bullying stopped. Craig Weatherall had been moved into 1C. That made a hole in the middle of Steve Weir's gang and it began to fall apart. Terence Ackroyd still had a few goes at him, and one day managed to corner him behind the bike-sheds. Worm socked him one. ('You'll only have to do it once,' Frud had told him.) He was right too, the boy went off chunnering, and rubbing his jaw in a daze. Worm collected Patsy and walked home on air, staggered at his own daring. That was Ackroyd taken care of.

In early July Darnley Comprehensive held its heats for the great Race. So many children wanted to compete that the organizers could only take a limited number from each school. They chose the best, and Worm was one of them. He easily qualified, and when his heat was over he felt he'd hardly begun.

Three weeks later, when he ran in the Race itself, he thought his cup of happiness was full. He had come near the end, but he *had* finished the course, and Mr Gill had taken him on one side and said, 'Well done, Wrigley. Try again next year. You've got all the makings of a really fine runner.'

Then, at the end of August, he got a letter in a long cream-coloured envelope, with the Darnley coat of arms on the flap. It was from the Town Hall. It said a recommendation had been made to them, by a Mr Richard Baxter, and at a special meeting of the councillors it had been decided that an award for bravery was to be made to Peter Wrigley, for his outstanding courage and clear-thinking, in saving the life of Paul Baxter, on Great Easemere Pike.

The final details hadn't yet been sorted out but it was hoped the award would be made at Worm's school prize-giving, in September, by Mr William Micklethwaite.

Worm read the letter three times then collapsed in a chair. It was Patsy who got it out of his hand and read it aloud to Mum and Auntie Glad. It took his mother a few minutes to recover. She sagged down next to Worm, and her eyes filled with tears.

Auntie Glad was much more practical. She was already discussing what they could all wear, with Patsy, and wondering where she could buy a hat.

Worm's eye caught sight of the *Darnley Examiner* lying on the table. There was a photo of Billy Micklethwaite on the front page, opening a new swimming-pool near Burnley. He looked at it carefully.

'Here he is, Mum, this is Billy Micklethwaite.' He felt nervous already.

'He came to your school, didn't he? He looks quite nice in this picture.'

'He's very big,' Worm muttered. 'He was an Olympic hurdler. Just look at him, he's about ten feet tall. I'm going to look daft, meeting him. I'll only come up to his knees.'

'Oh, you'll shoot up soon, you'll have grown by then.' Mrs Wrigley had endless faith in Worm.

'But Mum, it's next *month*.'

Darnley Comprehensive had grown so big that they couldn't fit everybody into the hall, for Speech Day. For this, the most boring event in the school year, they used a place in the town centre.

Albert Platt had made a fortune out of cotton, but he'd been generous with his money. He was a kind of Victorian Dickie Baxter. In Darnley you could walk in the Albert Platt Gardens, and swim in the Albert

166

Platt Public Baths. But there was nothing quite like the Albert Platt Memorial Hall. It was huge, it was grotesque, like a big sooty wedding cake dumped right in the middle of Darnley, with all the traffic whizzing round it.

Inside there was room for hundreds of people. On the platform at the front was a great organ, and a grand piano. Dusty chandeliers hung down from the ceiling, dozens of them, all big, all ugly. Worth a packet, so they said.

Under one of these, at two o'clock one afternoon at the end of September, sat Worm, waiting for the prizegiving to begin. He'd already got butterflies about going up on to that platform, and his presentation was right at the end. There was the whole of Speech Day to sit through first, and they hadn't even started yet.

Worm was in 2P now, and sitting next to Mr Potter, his new form master. Steve Weir sat next to him, so the teacher could bat him one, if he started anything.

In front of 2P were five rows of first years, then two rows of VIPs. The school had filed in last, when all the visitors were seated, so he couldn't see his mother. The senior staff and the school governors were up on the platform behind banks of flowers. So was Billy Micklethwaite, in a snappy blue suit. He'd agreed to give out the prizes, as well as the special award. In for a penny, in for a pound, he thought gloomily, as Mrs Heatherington, the senior music teacher, sat down at the piano. He'd make his own speech brief. That'd speed things up a bit.

Worm took in little of what was happening. He felt too nervous. Why couldn't he have gone up at the beginning? Why put him through this torture? It was going on and on.

The school orchestra played three long pieces (bad); the senior choir sang a couple of songs (worse); people with brains trotted smugly up and down the steps, collecting prizes, certificates, and silver cups; the speeches were filled with words like 'duty', 'persistence' and 'team spirit'.

It all washed over Worm like warm treacle. He'd gone beyond nerves now, into a kind of floating never-never land. So when Mr Potter whispered, 'Are you ready, Wrigley? Your turn coming up,' he jerked violently into life like something half-baked. Mrs Heatherington was playing the opening bars of the school song. This was his cue. He got to his feet and tried to join in, but his mouth was as dry as paper.

They'd spent all last week practising this song. It was partly in Latin. Mrs Heatherington hadn't got very far with 2P. 'Make the words clear,' she'd told them. 'Sing out... "This noise that men call fame, This dross that men call gold." What does "dross" mean?'

'Rubbish, Miss.'

'Quite right, Hudd. "This *rubbish* men call gold." One, two, and—Terence Ackroyd, give me that chewing-gum. What? No, you may not go to the lavatory... *and* "Non nobis, Domine." *Open your mouths.*'

Worm felt sorry for her, teaching songs in Latin to 2P. No wonder she was murdering that piano.

'This dross that men call gold,' Mr Potter boomed in his ear. What a funny song. Wonder what Albert Platt would have thought of that bit? 'This noise that

168

men call fame.' That's what Worm had wanted, in a way. Now it had come, he wasn't sure he liked it.

'And now,' Mr Fothergill was saying, 'before you all go home, I'm going to ask Mr Micklethwaite to make a very special presentation.'

Oh heck, Worm thought. Why did I ever come? The blood beat in his ears and he heard only bits of what the head was saying: 'Courage', 'pluck', 'stuck at his post' floated down to him, through the greenery. This was a bit different from the usual Speech Day garbage; and it was about him.

'So come along, Wrigley,' he heard.

It wasn't time for him to go up there already, surely?

But it was. Mr Potter was pushing him forward gently and as he left his seat Steve Weir leaned over and said grudgingly, 'Good luck, Pete.'

Well he was all right these days, Peter Wrigley was, growing up a bit. Not clever, but quite arty. He was helping paint scenery for the school play. Weir envied him that. You could stay in at dinner-time, in the warm. And he'd run in the Race too, so he must be good. Steve Weir hadn't even got through the heats.

All eyes were on Worm as he walked across the hall and climbed up the steps on to the platform. He looked great. All his clothes were new, even his underwear and his socks. Everything fitted; nothing smelt of fish and chips.

He began to walk across the platform, his eyes straight ahead, his face concrete with nerves. Then he stumbled over a microphone wire.

There was a slight ripple in the audience and a

snigger or two at the back, as Worm picked himself up again. The head looked down at his polished shoes and blushed. Rescues a boy from certain death, then trips over a perishing wire. What was he doing, for heaven's sake?

But Worm kept his cool. He brushed his trousers down, took a little breath to calm himself, then walked up to Billy. The Albert Platt Memorial Hall was deadly quiet now.

Mr Mickelthwaite shook him warmly by the hand, and gave him a scroll, tied with ribbon. Then he bent down and pinned a small bronze medallion on his blazer. The boy wasn't very big but he looked wiry, and quite strong. There was a seriousness about him that Billy liked. Here was a boy who knew what he wanted out of life, and would do his best to get it. The face was dimly familiar. A boy like this had been involved in that silly fire-bell business, back in the spring. It couldn't be this lad, surely?

The head was also looking at Worm. He'd come on a lot in the last few months. He'd filled out a bit, and there was colour in his cheeks. Even the hair seemed to have thickened up a fraction. Perhaps his mother was putting something on it.

At last Worm turned round and faced the audience. Now it was over he had the confidence to look down into the hall. He saw Mum, Patsy, and Auntie Glad in the front row with all the VIPs. He waved his certificate at them, and they all waved back. Behind them, another group of special visitors waved too.

He looked more carefully. 'Jolly good, splendid,' a familiar voice was saying, and there was the woman

Gert, looking like a battleship in a billowing spotted dress. Dot sat next to her, grinning broadly, and Millicent was in the next seat, dignified, pink, and pleased. On Gert's other side sat Brian Blake with his two sons. They were all in dark suits, looking very clean and scrubbed. Action Man was quietly beaming up at Worm and mouthing, 'Well done.'

The clapping went on and on. People stamped their feet. Vi Baxter cried, Mum cried, Auntie Glad cried and clapped louder than ever. She'd always known their Peter was made of the right stuff. He was like his dad. He was a little belter.

There was a reception afterwards, for all the VIPs. Worm went with his mother, Auntie Glad, and Patsy, but Dickie Baxter had managed to wangle two extra invitations for Pig and Frud as well.

'What did Billy Micklethwaite say to you, Worm?' Pig said jealously, through a mouthful of meringue. He hadn't improved. Still the same old Pig. 'Don't suppose he said much, did he?'

'Yes, he did,' Worm answered.

'Well, *what*?'

Worm said nothing at first, he was so used to people like Pig Baxter sneering at him.

'Go on, get on with it. What did he *say*?'

'Just that it was his lucky day, meeting me.'

'You're kidding.'

'I'm not. He said Mr Fothergill had told us how lucky we were, that he'd been able to come and everything, but that really, he was the lucky one.'

'Gedoff! I don't believe you.' Pig snaffled another meringue, and walked off.

But it was true. Well-known personalities like Billy Micklethwaite have to do so many boring things, like going round sports centres and opening bazaars. They don't often meet people like Peter Wrigley. There are only one or two people like him in any generation.

Now and again, once a year perhaps, someone comes along who is truly brave. That year it was Worm.

Also available from Lion Publishing:

No More School
Meg Harper

> 'I feel thick at school. The other kids tease me
> 'cos I live on a boat. You always have to do
> what the teachers say, even if you think it's
> really stupid... I just hate it!'

Flora loves living on a canal boat, but she loathes
school. So her best friend Joss covers for her when
she bunks off. Perfect. Then something happens to
change everything—Flora makes a new friend, Tan.
And soon she has a very big secret.

Meanwhile, Joss becomes strangely distant and
preoccupied. Is she jealous of Tan? Or is there
something more sinister going on?

ISBN 0 7459 3963 5

THE PECKHAM ANGELS ADVENTURES
Hilary Brand

Ossie the Ghostbuster

'Ossie's heart was thumping. His legs had
turned to plasticine. The sky was darkening
fast. All the angels looked fierce now. All the
cherubs looked sad. All the graves seemed
about to open and spill out horrid unnameable
contents...'

After school bully Wayne Grobbit forces Ossie
Johnson to go into Crown Hill Cemetery one night,
Ossie swears to get his revenge.
    This fast-moving, often funny story tells how
Ossie, with the help of his friends the Peckham
Angels, gets his own back on bullying Wayne and
solves a long-hidden family mystery.

ISBN 0 7459 4052 8

Lee the Jewel Thief

Lee is in trouble. His only hope is to replace his
mother's lost ring. Then everything will be all right.
Or will it?
    This second Peckham Angels story is fast, funny
and surprising, as Lee finds out that happy endings
are possible, even after his plans go badly wrong.

ISBN 0 7459 4053 6

All Lion books are available from your local
bookshop, or can be ordered direct from Lion
Publishing. For a free catalogue, showing the
complete list of titles available, please contact:

Customer Services Department
Lion Publishing plc
Peter's Way
Sandy Lane West
Oxford OX4 6HG

Tel: (01865) 747669
Fax: (01865) 715152

Our website can be found at:
www.lion-publishing.co.uk